Mother Goose Rhyme Time

Animals

Kimberly K. Faurot

Illustrated by Steve Cox

Musical Notations by Sara L. Waters

Fort Atkinson, Wisconsin
www.upstartbooks.com

Acknowledgments
Saroj Ghoting, Early Literacy Consultant

Special thanks to the following individuals and institutions:
Brad Kruse
Steve Cox
Sara L. Waters
Kristi McNellis
Lyle and JoAnne Faurot
Cathy Norris and the Children's Department staff, past and present,
of the Hedberg Public Library, Janesville, WI
Beth Murray
Carmel Clay Public Library Children's Department, Carmel, IN
Dr. Shirley Fitzgibbons
Jim Peitzman
Ann Denton
St. Paul Public Library, St. Paul, MN
University of Minnesota Libraries

All Highsmith/Upstart staff who worked on this project, including:
Matt Mulder, Publisher
Michelle McCardell, Managing Editor
Heidi Green, Art Director
Joann Lueck, Graphic Designer
Matt Napier, Production Designer
Sandy Harris, Product Development Manager

Published by UpstartBooks
W5527 State Road 106
P.O. Box 800
Fort Atkinson, Wisconsin 53538-0800
1-800-448-4887

Text © Kimberly K. Faurot, 2006
Illustrations © Steve Cox, 2006

The paper used in this publication meets the minimum requirements of American National Standard for Information Science—Permanence of Paper for Printed Library Material. ANSI/NISO Z39.48-1992.

All rights reserved. Printed in the United States of America.
The purchase of this book entitles the individual librarian or teacher to reproduce copies for use in the library or classroom. The reproduction of any part for an entire school system or for commercial use is strictly prohibited. No form of this work may be reproduced or transmitted or recorded without written permission from the publisher.

Contents

Introduction

Each Mother Goose Rhyme Time book is designed as a companion to a large size Mother Goose poster and character set. The books enhance the characters' possibilities by providing brief histories of each rhyme, simple musical notations so the rhymes may be played and sung, and suggestions for successfully incorporating the rhymes into library storytimes or classroom lessons.

Before You Begin

Punch out, laminate, and assemble the character cutouts as directed on the punch-out pages. Create an organized storage system so each poster and its accompanying pieces are easily accessible and safe from damage.

Why Nursery Rhymes?

Researchers have determined that young children who know nursery rhymes have a distinct advantage over those who do not as they embark upon the journey toward literacy (Bryant, Bradley, MacLean, and Crossland 426).

Nursery rhymes specifically foster and enhance:

- Acquisition of new vocabulary and concepts

- Oral language abilities, including the internalization of characteristic speech rhythms and intonation patterns

- Phonological awareness/sensitivity, the ability to recognize that spoken words consist of sound segments

- Sensitivity to and ability to detect rhyme and alliteration

Targeted nursery rhyme activities may additionally be used to help develop memorization skills, narrative skills and sequencing, print motivation, print awareness and tracking, and letter knowledge.

The linguistic routines inherent in nursery rhymes provide opportunities for children to hear sound similarities and differences, consequently developing and enhancing their phonological skills (MacLean, Bryant, and Bradley 277). In turn, phonological awareness is a key factor in eventual mastery of reading and spelling. This awareness of the smaller sounds in words does not develop automatically, in contrast to speech perception abilities, which are typically natural and spontaneous (National Research Council 51–57). Encouraging these phonological skills through introduction to rhyme and alliteration helps establish a foundation for effective decoding, and ultimately is a critical skill for fluent reading later on.

Early Literacy

Nursery rhymes are one of the building blocks of early literacy, a perspective that emphasizes skill development through young children's positive interactions with books and with caregivers, and regular exposure to literacy-rich environments and experiences. Early literacy does not mean teaching actual reading earlier, but laying a firm foundation for reading later on (Zero to Three). As MacLean, Bryant, and Bradley note, "… children acquire phonological awareness a long time before learning to read, through experiences which at the time have nothing to do with reading" (278). Activities such as chewing on and handling books, looking at and pointing to storybook pictures, saying rhymes and singing songs, rudimentary recognition of and interest in letters of the alphabet, and scribbling all help establish a child's preliminary foundation of knowledge about reading and writing long before he or she is developmentally ready to actually read or write. Just as a baby's babbling is a precursor to formal speech, these and other early literacy behaviors are precursors to reading (Project ECLIPSE).

For All Ages

Nursery rhymes are ideal components of programs for very young children, who respond naturally to the verses' engaging meter. The rhymes' brevity makes them well suited to short attention spans, and their bounceable, jumpable, clappable rhythms make them helpful tools in engaging active young listeners.

Despite this natural affinity, many children are not introduced to nursery rhymes as infants or preschoolers, and consequently require formal exposure upon reaching school. As children grow, nursery rhymes can play a shifting yet vital role in their literacy development. Incorporating rhymes into storytimes and activities for older children can establish confidence in "reading" a rhyme that is already comfortable and known; enhance phonological awareness and subsequently reading abilities; and provide a springboard for lessons in such diverse subjects as math, punctuation, creative writing, and history. Comparing the illustrations from various versions of Mother Goose can develop visual literacy, and research techniques may be taught through investigating the rhymes' possible origins. Older children can reminisce about the wording of rhymes that they remember from their own early years, and then compare those versions to the many different adaptations available.

Nursery rhymes are similarly effective in the elementary ESL/ELL (English as a Second Language/English Language Learners) classroom, supplying interesting characters, opportunities for vocabulary development, and plenty of action. The rhymes' natural rhythms help students develop an understanding of English speech cadences and intonation, as they do with very young children just beginning to utilize spoken language. Since most cultures have their own traditional play rhymes and songs, students can share and teach these in their native language to classmates and teachers. Cultural rhymes, games, and songs can also provide an ideal venue for parent/caregiver involvement with a child's class, and for affirming the vital importance of each student's cultural identity. Assignments may include children learning traditional rhymes at home to subsequently share in school or as part of a special presentation for

family members. Parents or caregivers can be invited to attend the class as visiting instructors to teach rhymes and songs from their own childhoods, encouraging appreciation for and recognition of their family's history.

In addition to the rhythms and phonological connections that nursery rhymes help promote, educators recognize that children must be familiar with the rhymes' content and meaning to understand many cultural allusions and references throughout their lives.

How to Use this Book

Utilize the sections of Mother Goose Rhyme Time that work best for you and your storytime group or classroom. Experiment with new ideas and techniques. Practice ahead of time so you feel comfortable with the material and can focus on the audience rather than on trying to remember how you intended to share the rhyme. Consider introducing "Mother Goose Rhyme Time" each week with a Mother Goose puppet or special song to signal what will happen next. For example:

> *(Tune: "The Farmer in the Dell")*
> It's time for Mother Goose
> I've heard she's on the loose!
> She'll bring a rhyme for storytime,
> It's time for Mother Goose!

Each chapter includes the following sections:

Rhyme

A standard version of the nursery rhyme, which matches the poster included in the companion set.

Variants

Alternate wording or versions of the rhyme that are different from the version in this book.

History

A brief historical note about the rhyme's possible origins. Occasionally sharing bits of background information can add to the rhyme's charm and entertainment value for parents and caregivers as they find themselves inevitably reading it repeatedly with their child! The references may also be used as a familiar and engaging entry to older students' history lessons.

Musical Notation

Simple, storytime-tested melodies for each rhyme, with autoharp/guitar chords. Tunes reflect standard melodies if any are known, and offer straightforward new adaptations for rhymes with obscure historical tunes.

Preparing and Using the Mother Goose Rhyme Time Pieces

A list of the rhyme pieces and the poster are needed for presenting each rhyme, with preliminary preparation and presentation suggestions. For example, before sharing the rhyme, place the poster on an easel so the audience can see it clearly. For some rhymes, pieces may be stacked in reverse order of appearance and hidden out of sight before the audience arrives. Rhyme pieces may be held in the presenter's hands, glued or taped securely to a paint stirrer and held aloft, or affixed to a large Velcro or magnet board. If you wish to incorporate motions or use a musical instrument for accompaniment, point to each piece on the board in turn as you lead the group in the actions or play and sing the song.

Storytime

Ideas for sharing the nursery rhyme as a song or chant, with suggestions for various ways to repeat it. Sing or say the rhyme quickly and slowly, loudly and quietly, while bouncing, patting your lap, or clapping to keep a rhythm. Add movements and animal noises or snoring as desired, mimicking the action in the rhyme. Encourage the children's caregivers to adapt movements or make up new ones as appropriate for their child. Possible motions for babies and older children are included. Share one rhyme several times during a single storytime, and repeat the same rhyme over several storytimes.

Early Literacy Activities

These activities follow the seven focus areas recommended in Every Child Ready to Read @

Your Library, an early literacy partnership project between the Public Library Association and the Association for Library Service to Children, divisions of the American Library Association, and the National Institute of Child Health and Human Development (NICHD) of the National Institutes of Health (see www.pla.org/earlyliteracy.htm). A clear overview of these focus areas as well as innovative activity suggestions are included in *Early Literacy Storytimes @ Your Library* by Saroj Nadkarni Ghoting and Pamela Martin-Diaz (American Library Assn., 2006).

Consider integrating several (not all) of the Early Literacy Activities or techniques suggested below as you share the nursery rhyme. All activities should be approached in a fun and playful manner, encouraging curiosity and allowing for children's individual differences. Avoid any tendencies toward drill or rote memorization (Yopp 702). **Note:** Be aware of children's developmental stages and focus on the activities that are appropriate to the ages and stages of your group. The suggestions provided are intended to give you a variety of ideas to work with over time. You will not incorporate all of the techniques into any one rhyme, or even all into one storytime. Try different activities to highlight a different skill during each storytime.

Print Motivation

- Encourage interest in and excitement about reading and books. Say the words rhythmically and with enthusiasm.

- Create voices for the characters, and change your tone and facial expression as appropriate to the context to convey your enjoyment of the rhyme.

- Repeat the rhyme several times together with the children, encouraging their own enjoyment and internalization of its lively rhythms.

Language and Vocabulary

- Introduce and explain new words or new meanings to familiar words. Use the rhyme pieces to illustrate, pointing to the pictures of the words you are saying or the events you are describing.

- Talk or sing about the illustrations: "I see a haystack." "I see a cow." Pause for the children to name the object to which you are pointing: "I see a _____." Expand on descriptive features of the illustrations to build vocabulary and encourage the children's awareness of and attention to details. For example: "I see a boy. A boy wearing a blue hat and blue clothes."

Phonological Awareness

- Play with rhymes, practice breaking words apart and putting them back together, and listen for beginning sounds and alliteration. Play with the words, objects, and names in the rhyme and change them (see each chapter for examples). Use puppets or props to dramatize the alternate word choices.

- Explain that rhyming words sound the same at the end, and give examples. Try pausing just before the end of a rhyming pair and encourage the children to supply the rhyming word with the support of visual clues or context, or simply through the sounds suggested by the rhyme.

- Play an "oddity task" game. For example, which word does not rhyme? Horn, sheep, corn. *(Answer: sheep.)* Which word sounds different at the beginning? Diddle, fiddle, dog. *(Answer: fiddle.)* Which word sounds different at the end? Cat, hat, dog. *(Answer: dog.)*

- Blend word parts in a variety of ways.

   Syllables: dump ... ling. What's the word? *(Dumpling.)*

   Onset sound: /d/ ... og. What's the word? *(Dog.)* What other words start with /d/? (Note that the symbol / / signifies the sound of the letter.)

   Phoneme by phoneme (for older children, in primary grades): /m/-/oo/-/n/. What's the word? *(Moon.)*

- Practice segmenting or "stretching" the nursery rhyme words (for older children, in primary grades). Show the children a rubber band and stretch it out and in. As you stretch the rubber band out longer, you can see all of its parts more clearly. Explain that you can also stretch words, so that you can hear each individual sound (phoneme) in the word. Stretch the word "on": /o/-/n/. Sometimes one phoneme is represented by more than one letter, such as in the name "John": /J/-/oh/-/n/. "John" contains three phonemes. Stretch other nursery rhyme words.

- Clap words: Clap once for each word in the rhyme, following the poster. Introduce variety by stomping feet or jumping once for each word.

- Clap syllables: Slightly older children can learn to clap once for each syllable in the rhyme. Practice with one word at a time as the children begin to understand the concept. For example: Did-dle (2 claps); Did-dle (2 claps); Dump-ling (2 claps); my (1 clap); son (1 clap); John (1 clap). Introduce variety by stomping feet or jumping to the syllables.

- Sing the nursery rhyme to its familiar tune. Follow the musical notations and autoharp/guitar chords provided if desired.

Print Awareness

- Help the children notice print, know how to handle books, and follow the written word on a page. Point to the poster included in the companion kit and say: "Our nursery rhyme is written right up here. I'll read it aloud, and then we'll say it again together." Follow the text of the rhyme with your finger as you read the poster, from left to right to reinforce print directionality as well as the concept that print stands for spoken language.

- Occasionally turn the poster upside down or sideways and see if the children detect the problem.

Narrative Skills

- Practice retelling stories or events with the children, sequencing the order in which events happened, and adding descriptions. Talk and ask open-ended questions about

the rhyme and the objects and characters in it, and allow the children to ask questions. Avoid asking yes/no questions unless there is a specific purpose in doing so. Qualify questions by including the phrase, "do you think," such as in "Why do you think ...?" or "What do you think ...?" This type of question does not have a "right" answer that children are afraid they will get wrong. Talk about ways in which we may have experiences or feelings that are similar to those of the nursery rhyme characters. For example, how do you think Little Boy Blue will feel when he wakes up and finds that the sheep are in the meadow and the cows are eating the corn?

- If you have a small enough group and adequate time, act out the rhyme with creative dramatics. Make sure each child gets to play all of the roles if possible, and to choose who or what they want to be.

- Consider incorporating craft activities into the program as a springboard for the children to retell rhymes and stories. (See "Take-home Rhyme Pieces" and "Additional Extension Ideas" in each chapter.)

- As the children's repertoire of nursery rhyme friends grows, ask "Who am I?" nursery rhyme riddles. For example: "I blow my horn to call the sheep and the cows. I fell asleep under a haystack. Who am I?" (*Answer: Little Boy Blue.*)

Letter Knowledge

- Help the children learn to recognize and identify letters; to know that they have different names and sounds; and to understand that the same letter can look different. Begin with letter sounds that young children can articulate easily, and introduce the sounds in the general order they develop in children's speech. (See www.pla.org/ala/pla/plaissues/earlylit/workshops parent/lettersounds.pdf.)

Choose word examples that correspond to the letter sounds. For example, "S is for Sock." Avoid word examples such as "S is for

Sheep," which begins with the "sh" sound rather than a hard "s."

Introduce this group of letters first, one at a time, though not necessarily in this order:

B, M, D, T, W, P, N, Y, H

Introduce this group of letters next:

S, F, G, V, Z, K, C

Introduce this group of letters last:

L, R, J

Parent/Caregiver Connection

- Reinforce the parent/caregiver's key role in their child's early literacy development through comfortable, relaxed times together with songs, rhymes, and books.

- Encourage parents/caregivers to participate during storytime and to incorporate nursery rhymes at home during play and reading times. Select one of the early literacy activities that you share together during storytime, and briefly explain how the activity supports children's early literacy development. Suggest repeating the activity at home. Try different activities to highlight different skills during each storytime.

- Share information about Dialogic, or "Hear and Say" Reading (see Resources). Encourage parents and caregivers to individually discuss the day's rhyme, its characters, and events in an open-ended way with their children, following the child's interest while affirming and expanding upon their answers. Build on the things that catch the child's interest. This type of positive, interactive discussion around familiar rhymes and books helps improve early language development, communication, and parent/child relationships.

- Share brief facts about the direct benefits of reading to children and of playing word games with them.

- Model enthusiastic reading behaviors and interactions, emphasizing fun and enjoyment as the goals.

Take-home Rhyme Pieces

- Distribute take-home card stock illustrations of the day's nursery rhyme (included in each rhyme chapter), and either color and assemble them at the end of storytime or encourage the families to do so at home. Make a sample of the take-home version, and demonstrate singing or saying the rhyme using the small-size piece(s). (Families may affix sticky-back magnet material to pieces for playtime use on a magnetic surface such as a cookie sheet or the refrigerator if desired. Be aware of choking hazard considerations for younger children.)

Additional Extension Ideas

- Make companion crafts for the day's nursery rhyme, providing materials for both children and adults, or share storybooks extending the rhyme's theme, content, or concepts.

- Display nursery rhyme and children's poetry books and make them available for your audience to borrow and share at home. Emphasize that the books don't need to be read from cover to cover. Encourage children and their caregivers to take turns selecting poems and rhymes as they read, and to talk about details of illustrations that accompany the text. Show pictures from several different nursery rhyme books that illustrate the day's nursery rhyme, and repeat the rhyme together with each new illustration. Some classic and favorite Mother Goose books are listed in the bibliography.

- Build a nursery rhyme village, make a giant map of Mother Goose Town, orchestrate a Mother Goose Musical performance, or celebrate International Mother Goose Day (May 1).

- Let your creativity run wild, and have fun!

The ideas detailed in this volume, together with the nursery rhyme poster and character set from the companion kit, provide tools and techniques to help you successfully weave nursery rhymes and related activities into the fabric of your storytimes and curriculum. I hope that these methods will help you gain confidence and facility in sharing nursery rhymes, and also provide you with a deeper understanding of the enduring benefits afforded by actively sharing this rich tradition with your children, their families, and caregivers.

References

Nursery Rhymes and Early Literacy

Adams, Marilyn Jager. *Beginning to Read: Thinking and Learning About Print.* MIT Press, 1990.

Blevins, Wiley. *Phonemic Awareness Activities for Early Reading Success: Easy, Playful Activities That Prepare Children for Phonics Instruction.* Scholastic Professional Books, 1997.

Bryant, P. E., and L. Bradley, M. MacLean, J. Crossland. "Nursery Rhymes, Phonological Skills and Reading." *Journal of Child Language,* 16.2 (1989): 407–428.

Bryant, P. E., M. MacLean, L. L. Bradley, and J. Crossland. (1990). "Rhyme and Alliteration, Phoneme Detection, and Learning to Read." *Developmental Psychology,* 26.3 (1990): 429–438.

Fox, Mem. *Reading Magic: Why Reading Aloud to Our Children Will Change their Lives Forever.* Harcourt, 2001.

Geller, Linda Gibson. "Children's Rhymes and Literacy Learning: Making Connections." *Language Arts,* 60.2 (1983): 184–193.

Ghoting, Saroj Nadkarni, and Pamela Martin-Diaz. *Early Literacy Storytimes @ Your Library: Partnering with Caregivers for Success.* American Library Assn., 2006.

Hempenstall, Kerry. "The Role of Phonemic Awareness in Beginning Reading: A Review." *Behaviour Change,* 14 (1997): 201–214.

The International Reading Association and the National Association for the Education of Young Children. *Learning to Read and Write: Developmentally Appropriate Practices for Young Children.* www.naeyc.org/about/positions/pdf/PSREAD98.PDF. 1998.

Kirtley, Clare, Peter Bryant, Morag MacLean, and Lynette Bradley. "Rhyme, Rime, and the Onset of Reading." *Journal of Experimental Child Psychology,* 48 (1989): 224–245.

MacLean, Morag, Peter Bryant, and Lynette Bradley. "Rhymes, Nursery Rhymes, and Reading in Early Childhood." *Merrill-Palmer Quarterly,* 33.3 (1987): 255–281.

Morrow, Lesley Mandel. *Getting Ready to Read with Mother Goose.* Sadlier-Oxford, 2001.

Morrow, Lesley Mandel. *Literacy Development in the Early Years: Helping Children Read and Write.* 4th ed. Allyn & Bacon, 2001.

National Research Council. Catherine Snow, M. Susan Burns, and Peg Griffin, eds. *Preventing Reading Difficulties in Young Children.* National Academy Press, 1998.

Project ECLIPSE. "Mother Goose: A Scholarly Exploration." 31 Dec. 2005. www.eclipse.rutgers.edu/goose/literacy/.

Sadlier-Oxford. "Nursery Rhymes and Phonemic Awareness." Professional Development Series, Volume 3. Sadlier-Oxford, 2000.

Yopp, Hallie Kay. "Developing Phonemic Awareness in Young Children." *The Reading Teacher,* 45.9 (1992): 696–703.

Zero to Three. "Brain Wonders: Early Literacy." 31 Dec. 2005. www.zerotothree.org/brainwonders/EarlyLiteracy.html.

Baa Baa Black Sheep

"Baa baa, black sheep,

Have you any wool?"

"Yes sir, yes sir,

Three bags full.

One for my master,

And one for my dame,

And one for the little boy

Who lives down the lane."

Variants

The words of this rhyme have remained fairly consistent over the years, with the occasional variation of "one for the little boy who cries in the lane." Early versions also use "Yes merry have I" in place of "Yes sir, yes sir."

Some modern adaptations of the rhyme and song include Raffi's "Cluck, Cluck, Red Hen" on *The Corner Grocery Store* (MCA Records, 1979) and "Baa Baa Black Sheep" / "Baa Baa White Sheep" on *Singable Songs for the Very Young* (Troubador Records Ltd., 1976).

The song is also commonly adapted by singing it twice, substituting "one for the little girl who lives down the lane" the second time through.

History

More than 250 years old, "Baa Baa Black Sheep" was included in *Tommy Thumb's Pretty Song Book,* which was published in England around 1744 and is the earliest known book of nursery rhymes. Thought to be a complaint by the sheep farmers against the export tax imposed on wool in 1275, the song refers to paying both the master (the king) and the dame (the nobility, or possibly the Church). Some early versions such as that in *Mother Goose's Melody* (c. 1765) darkly assert: "But none for the little boy who cries in the lane" (i.e., the sheep farmers).

Musical Notation

See musical notation on page 19.

Preparing and Using the Mother Goose Rhyme Time Pieces

"Baa Baa Black Sheep" pieces:

- Black sheep

- Bag 1

- Bag 2

- Bag 3

- "Baa Baa Black Sheep" poster

Organize the "Baa Baa Black Sheep" rhyme pieces ahead of time in the order in which they appear in the rhyme: stack the three bags on top of each other with the sheep on the very top. Hide the stack out of sight.

Before sharing the rhyme, place the poster on an easel so the audience can see it clearly. Hold the sheep in one hand as you sing the rhyme. With your other hand, hold up each bag and then put it down again as you sing, or affix the bags successively to a large Velcro or magnet board. If you wish to incorporate motions or use a musical instrument for accompaniment, place all of the pieces on the board and point to each in turn as you lead the group in the actions or play and sing the song.

Utilize the sections of Mother Goose Rhyme Time that work best for you and your storytime group or classroom. Experiment with new ideas and techniques. Practice ahead of time so you feel comfortable with the material and can focus on the audience rather than on trying to remember how you intended to share the rhyme.

Storytime

Sing "Baa Baa Black Sheep" while rocking back and forth or clapping to keep a gentle rhythm. Sing the rhyme quickly and slowly, loudly and quietly. Incorporate movements as desired. Share the song several times, changing the little "boy" to little "girl" the second time through.

Babies (*Sitting on caregivers' laps*)

"Baa baa, black sheep,
(*Rock baby throughout song.*)
Have you any wool?"
"Yes sir, yes sir,
(*Nod head.*)
Three bags full.
(*Hold up three fingers.*)
One for my master,
(*Hold up one finger.*)
And one for my dame,
(*Hold up one finger.*)
And one for the little boy
(*Hold up one finger.*)
Who lives down the lane."

Older Children (*Sitting or standing*)

"Baa baa, black sheep,
(*Sway back and forth throughout song, or clap hands rhythmically.*)
Have you any wool?"
(*Hands out, questioningly.*)
"Yes sir, yes sir,
(*Nod head.*)
Three bags full.
(*Hold up three fingers.*)
One for my master,
(*Hold up one finger.*)
And one for my dame,
(*Hold up one finger.*)
And one for the little boy
(*Hold up one finger.*)
Who lives down the lane."

Early Literacy Activities

Consider integrating one or several of the activities or techniques suggested below as you share the nursery rhyme. All activities should be approached in a fun and playful manner, encouraging curiosity and allowing for children's individual differences. **Note:** Be aware of children's developmental stages and focus on the activities that are appropriate for the ages and stages of your group. The suggestions provided are intended to give you a variety of ideas to work with over time. You will not incorporate all of the techniques at once. Share one rhyme several times during a single storytime, and repeat the same rhyme over several storytimes. Try different activities to highlight a different skill during each storytime.

Print Motivation (*Encourage interest in and excitement about reading and books.*)

- Say the words rhythmically and with enthusiasm, conveying your enjoyment of the rhyme.

- Create a baa-ing voice for the sheep, and change your tone and facial expression as appropriate to the context.

- Repeat the rhyme several times together with the children, encouraging their own enjoyment and internalization of its lively rhythms.

Language and Vocabulary (*Introduce and explain new words or new meanings to familiar words.*)

- Use the rhyme pieces to illustrate and help explain language and vocabulary. Say: "We are talking to a sheep (*point to the sheep*), so we start out by greeting her in her own language. What does a sheep say? 'Baa baa!' What color is this sheep? She's a black sheep. We are asking her if she has any wool. Wool is the soft curly hair that is a sheep's coat all over its body. A sheep's wool grows during the summer, fall, and winter and becomes very heavy. In the springtime, sheep have their wool sheared, or cut off." If possible, show the children some real sheep's wool. Pass it around so they can feel it. "The sheep in our rhyme had lots of wool—three bags full! Let's count the bags of wool (*hold up or point to each bag in turn*)—one, two, three! One bag is for her master, who is maybe the farmer, and one bag is for the dame, which means a lady. Maybe she is the farmer's wife. The third bag is for a little boy who lives down the lane, or down the road."

- Talk or sing about the illustrations: "I see a sheep." "I see a bag of wool." Pause for the children to name the object to which you are pointing: "I see a _____." Expand on descriptive features of the illustrations to build vocabulary and encourage the children's awareness of and attention to details: "I see a sheep. A sheep with curly black hair and four legs."

Phonological Awareness (*Play with rhymes, practice breaking words apart and putting them back together, and listen for beginning sounds and alliteration.*)

- Play with the words, colors, animals, and objects in the rhyme and change them. Use puppets or props to dramatize. Be creative, such as:

  "Neigh neigh, blue horse,
  Will you carry me?"
  "Yes ma'am, yes ma'am,
  As far as you can see.
  Gallop to the playground, gallop home
      for lunch;

  Gallop to the library, it's time to read
      a bunch."

- Explain that rhyming words sound the same at the end. "Wool" and "full"; "me" and "see"; and "lunch" and "bunch" are all rhyming word pairs. Change the characters to whom the sheep would give her wool in the song. For example: "One for my mother, / And one for my dad. / One for the little dog / Who looks kind of sad." Try pausing just before the end of a rhyming pair and encourage the children to supply the rhyming word (such as "sad" above) with the support of visual clues or context, or simply through the sounds suggested by the rhyme.

- Play an "oddity task" game. For example, which word does not rhyme? Wool, sheep, full. (*Answer: sheep.*) Which word sounds different at the beginning? Black, bags, dame. (*Answer: dame.*)

- Blend word parts in a variety of ways.

  Syllables: mas … ter. What's the word? (*Master.*)

  Onset sound: /b/ … oy. What's the word? (*Boy.*) What other words start with /b/?

  Phoneme by phoneme (for older children, in primary grades): /b/-/a/-/g/-/s/. What's the word? (*Bags.*)

- Practice segmenting or "stretching" the nursery rhyme words (for older children, in primary grades). Show the children a rubber band and stretch it out and in. As you stretch the rubber band out longer, you can see all of its parts more clearly. Explain that you can also stretch words, so that you can hear each individual sound (phoneme) in the word. Stretch the word "bags": /b/-/a/-/g/-/s/. Sometimes one phoneme is represented by more than one letter, such as in the word "sheep": /sh/-/ee/-/p/. "Sheep" contains three phonemes. Stretch other nursery rhyme words.

- Clap words: Clap once for each word in the rhyme, following the poster. Introduce variety by stomping feet or jumping once for each word.

- Clap syllables: Older children can learn to clap once for each syllable in the rhyme. Practice with one word at a time as the children begin to understand the concept. For example: Baa (1 clap); baa (1 clap); black (1 clap); sheep (1 clap); have (1 clap); you (1 clap); an-y (2 claps) wool (1 clap)? Introduce variety by stomping feet or jumping to the syllables.

Print Awareness *(Notice print and know how to handle books and follow the written word on a page.)*

- Point to the "Baa Baa Black Sheep" poster. Say: "Our nursery rhyme is written right up here. I'll read it aloud, and then we'll say it again together." Follow the text of the rhyme with your finger as you read the poster, from left to right.

- Occasionally turn the poster upside down or sideways and see if the children detect the problem.

Narrative Skills *(Practice retelling stories or events, sequencing the order in which events happened, and adding descriptions.)*

- Talk and ask two or three open-ended questions about the rhyme and the objects and characters in it, and allow the children to ask questions. Avoid asking yes/no questions unless there is a specific purpose for doing so. Qualify questions by including the phrase "do you think," as in "Why do you think ...?" or "What do you think ...?" This type of question does not have a "right" answer that children are afraid they will get wrong. For example: What do you think each person who receives a bag of wool in our rhyme will do with it? Why do you think the sheep chose those three people to receive the wool? To whom do you think the sheep will give the wool to next time? Why?

- Talk about: What are the things that keep us warm? *(Blankets, sweaters, coats, mittens, and so forth.)*

- If you have a small enough group and adequate time, act out "Baa Baa Black Sheep" with creative dramatics. Have one group of children be the questioners, and the other

children reply as the sheep. Make sure that each child gets to play both roles.

Letter Knowledge—Letter B *(Learn to recognize and identify letters, knowing that they have different names and sounds and that the same letter can look different.)*

- Show a large-size cutout or magnet-backed foam letter "B" and "b" (see Resources). Point to the capital "B" letters that begin the words "Baa Baa," and "Black" in the title of your poster. Say: "Here is the letter B—a big uppercase, or capital B." Draw the capital letter "B" in the air as a group. Point to the small letter "b" on the poster within the rhyme's text. Say: "Here is also the letter b—a small, lowercase b." Draw a lowercase "b" in the air as a group. Make the /B/ sound and say: "B is for Baa Baa; B is for Black; B is for Boy; B is for Bed; B is for Ball; B is for Bike; B is for Bear; B is for Balloon; B is for Baby; B is for Book." Encourage the audience to repeat each phrase after you. Include three or four examples.

- Demonstrate making the shapes of "B" and "b" using string or pipe cleaners.

Parent/Caregiver Connection

- Reinforce the parent/caregiver's key role in their child's early literacy development through comfortable, relaxed times together with songs, rhymes, and books. Emphasize fun and enjoyment as the goals.

- Encourage caregivers to participate during storytime and to incorporate "Baa Baa Black Sheep" at home during play and reading times. Select one of the "Baa Baa Black Sheep" early literacy activities that you share together during storytime, and briefly explain how the activity supports children's early literacy development. Suggest repeating the activity at home. Try different activities to highlight different skills during each storytime.

- Share information about Dialogic, or "Hear and Say" Reading (see Resources). Encourage parents and caregivers to individually discuss the day's rhyme, its charac-

ters, and events in an open-ended way with their children, following the child's interest while affirming and expanding upon their answers. For example, point to the sheep in "Baa Baa Black Sheep" and ask, "What animal is this?" Child: "Lamb." Follow up with positive affirmation, and enlarge: "Yes, it's a grown-up lamb, which is a sheep. What do you notice about this sheep?" Child: "Eyes." Expand: "Yes, the sheep's eyes are closed." Help the child repeat longer phrases. Ask open-ended questions such as: "What do you see in this picture?" Build on the things that catch the child's interest. This type of positive, interactive discussion around familiar rhymes and books helps improve early language development, communication, and parent/child relationships.

Take-home "Baa Baa Black Sheep"

Copy the "Baa Baa Black Sheep" illustrations from pages 20–21 onto card stock and distribute. Color and cut out the pieces at the end of storytime, or encourage the families to do so at home. Make a sample of the take-home version, and demonstrate singing or saying the rhyme using the small pieces. (Families may affix sticky-back magnet material to pieces for playtime use on a magnetic surface such as a cookie sheet or the refrigerator if desired. Be aware of choking hazard considerations for younger children.)

Additional Extension Ideas

Note: For all craft activities, provide materials for adult attendees as well as children. Encourage children and adults to talk together about what they are making, and to use the completed crafts to retell or act out the rhyme.

- Show the pictures from several different nursery rhyme books that illustrate "Baa Baa Black Sheep," and repeat the rhyme together with each new illustration. Talk about the differences between the various illustrations.

- Talk about: For a sheep, being shorn is like a person getting a haircut. The sheep farmers shear the sheep in the springtime so the sheep will be cooler during the summer. Wearing their wool "sweaters" all summer would be very hot. Look at photographs of woolly sheep and shorn sheep.

- Talk about: What do we do with a sheep's wool after the sheep is shorn? Wash the wool; card it to get out the tangles; spin it into yarn; dye the yarn; and crochet, knit, or weave it into cloth. Show the children an old wool sweater from home or a second-hand store. If possible, unravel a portion of the sweater so they can see how the knitting goes together.

- Flatten large white basket coffee filters and mottle them with black and gray watercolor paints. Allow the filters to dry completely, then cut them into sheep body outlines. Cut heads and legs from black construction paper and affix with glue. Highlight facial features with white crayons or other crayons or pens that will show up on dark paper.

- Make a "Baa Baa Black Sheep" craft with a cutout black card stock or construction paper body and clip clothespin legs. Draw or glue a face, ears, and tail on the sheep. Decorate the body with bits of black yarn or curled pieces of black paper.

- Make Black Sheep Envelope Puppets that give wool. Complete instructions are included in *A Pocketful of Puppets: Mother Goose* by Tamara Hunt and Nancy Renfro (Nancy Renfro Studios, 1998).

- Talk about the various colors of sheep in real life: white, black, and gray. Imagine together what other colors pretend sheep could be. Make sheep outlines on colored paper and print the name of the color on each sheep. Sing "Baa Baa Black Sheep" with different colors or patterns, such as "Baa baa pink sheep," "Baa baa plaid sheep," and so forth.

- Change the amount of wool the sheep has and count the bags. Group the bags into sets and sing about them. For example, ... Yes sir, yes sir, / Ten bags full. / Three for my master, / And three for my dame, / And four for the little boy / Who lives down the

lane. Talk about: If the sheep had five bags of wool and could give them to absolutely anybody, to whom would she give each of them? How about ten bags?

- Sing additional verses about animals other than sheep and the contributions they share with us, or the things that they like. Listen to Raffi's lovely "Cluck, Cluck, Red Hen" on *The Corner Grocery Store* (MCA Records, 1979) or make up your own adaptations. It is fine to stick closely to the framework of the original song; rhyming is not essential to this activity. Discuss what kind of containers various items are packaged in when we buy them at the grocery store. For example, eggs typically come in cartons; milk comes in jugs or cartons or bottles; honey comes in a jar or a plastic honey bear; and so forth. Begin each verse with the animal's noise and what color it is, such as "Buzz buzz yellow bee"; "Moo moo brown cow"; "Cluck cluck red hen"; "Woof woof white dog"; and so forth. Have the children act out the verses with puppets and props.

"Buzz buzz yellow bee,
Have you any honey?"
"Yes ma'am, yes ma'am,
Three jars full.
One for my master
And one for my dame.
One for the little girl
Who lives down the lane."

- Share "Baa Baa Black Sheep" "in two voices" from *You Read to Me, I'll Read to You: Very Short Mother Goose Tales to Read Together* by Mary Ann Hoberman (Little, Brown and Company, 2005).

- Make the shapes of "B" and "b" using string, pipe cleaners, or clay.

Baa Baa Black Sheep

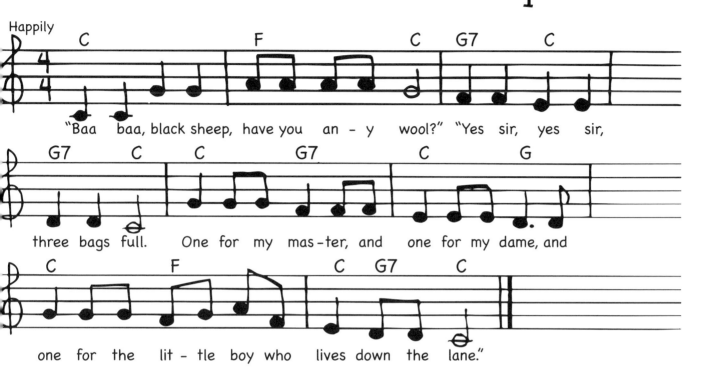

"Baa baa, black sheep, have you an - y wool?" "Yes sir, yes sir,

three bags full. One for my mas - ter, and one for my dame, and

one for the lit - tle boy who lives down the lane."

Take-home Baa Baa Black Sheep

"Baa baa, black sheep,
Have you any wool?"
"Yes sir, yes sir,
Three bags full.
One for my master,
And one for my dame,
And one for the little boy
Who lives down the lane."

Blow, Wind, Blow!

Blow, wind, blow!

And go, mill, go!

That the miller may grind his corn;

That the baker may take it,

And into bread make it,

And bring us a loaf in the morn.

Blow, wind, blow!

And go, mill go!

Variants

The earliest version of the rhyme read "And send us some hot in the morn" instead of "And bring us a loaf in the morn."

History

Little is written about this rhyme, even by the Opies. It first appeared in *Little Rhymes for Little Folk* in 1812. Less well known than many rhymes and without a commonly recognized tune, it was nevertheless included in L. E. Orth's *Sixty Songs from Mother Goose,* first published and performed in 1901.

Musical Notation

See musical notation on page 29.

Preparing and Using the Mother Goose Rhyme Time Pieces

"Blow, Wind, Blow!" pieces:

- Windmill body with attached arms

- Loaf of bread

- "Blow, Wind, Blow!" poster

Before sharing the rhyme, place the poster on an easel so the audience can see it clearly. Hold the windmill in one hand as you sing or say the rhyme, using your other hand to spin the windmill's arms around. Produce the baker's "loaf" on cue. If you wish to incorporate motions or use a musical instrument for accompaniment, affix the pieces to a large Velcro or magnet board. Point to the pieces and spin the windmill's arms as you lead the group in the actions or play and sing the song.

Utilize the sections of Mother Goose Rhyme Time that work best for you and your storytime group or classroom. Experiment with new ideas and techniques. Practice ahead of time so you feel comfortable with the material and can focus on the audience rather than on trying to remember how you intended to share the rhyme.

Storytime

Share "Blow, Wind, Blow!" as a song or as a chant; bouncing, patting your lap, or clapping to keep a rhythm. Sing or say the rhyme quickly and slowly, loudly and quietly. Incorporate movements as desired. Encourage the children's caregivers to adapt motions or make up new ones as appropriate for their child; many different actions are possible. Here are a few options:

Babies (*Sitting on caregivers' laps*)

> Blow, wind, blow!
> (*Gently blow baby's hair.*)
> And go, mill, go!
> (*Bicycle baby's legs.*)
> That the miller may grind his corn;
> (*Bounce baby.*)
> That the baker may take it,
> And into bread make it,
> (*Tickle baby's belly.*)
> And bring us a loaf in the morn.
> (*Bounce baby.*)
> Blow, wind, blow!
> (*Gently blow baby's hair.*)
> And go, mill go!
> (*Bicycle baby's legs.*)

Older Children (*Standing*)

> Blow, wind, blow!
> (*Blow with mouth; wave hands back and forth.*)
> And go, mill, go!
> (*Swivel arms like a windmill.*)
> That the miller may grind his corn;
> (*Pound fists.*)
> That the baker may take it,
> And into bread make it,
> (*Pretend to knead dough.*)
> And bring us a loaf in the morn.
> (*Rub belly.*)
> Blow, wind, blow!
> (*Blow with mouth; wave hands back and forth.*)
> And go, mill go!
> (*Swivel arms like a windmill.*)

Early Literacy Activities

Consider integrating several of the activities or techniques suggested below as you share the nursery rhyme. All activities should be approached in a fun and playful manner, encouraging curiosity and allowing for children's individual differences. **Note:** Be aware of children's developmental stages and focus on the activities that are appropriate for the ages and stages of your group. The suggestions provided are intended to give you a variety of ideas to work with over time. You will not incorporate all of the techniques at once. Share one rhyme several times during a single storytime, and repeat the same rhyme over several storytimes. Try different activities to highlight a different skill during each storytime.

Print Motivation (*Encourage interest in and excitement about reading and books.*)

- Say the words rhythmically and with enthusiasm, conveying your enjoyment of the rhyme.

- Repeat the rhyme several times together with the children, encouraging their own enjoyment and internalization of its lively rhythms.

Language and Vocabulary (*Introduce and explain new words or new meanings to familiar words.*)

- Use the rhyme pieces to illustrate and help explain language and vocabulary. Say: "We are telling the wind to blow! (*Blow with your mouth.*) When the wind blows, it makes the arms (*point to the windmill's arms*) of the windmill (*point to the entire windmill*) go around. The windmill is just called a 'mill' in our rhyme. Mills used to be the place where farmers would bring their wheat and corn to be ground into flour. We need flour to make bread and cake and cookies!" If possible, show the children an ear and kernels of corn, some cornmeal, and corn bread as well as wheat, flour, and whole-grain bread. If you have access to a flour grinder and wheat kernels (*both are sold at many health-food stores*), take turns grinding the grain into flour as a group. "The baker will bring us a loaf (*point to the loaf of bread*), which is a loaf of bread in the morn, which means in the morning. Morn is a shortened way of saying 'morning.'"

- Talk or sing about the illustrations: "I see a windmill." "I see a loaf of bread." Pause for the children to name the object to which you are pointing: "I see a _____." Expand on descriptive features of the illustrations to build vocabulary and encourage the children's awareness of and attention to details: "I see a windmill. A windmill with a blue roof and a red door."

Phonological Awareness (*Play with rhymes, practice breaking words apart and putting them back together, and listen for beginning sounds and alliteration.*)

- Echo the rhythm of the "Blow, Wind, Blow!" rhyme with the following chant:

  Bake, bread, bake.
  A sandwich we will make!
  With peanut butter and jelly, too,
  Bananas, apples,
  And chocolate goo!
  Bake, bread, bake.
  A sandwich we will make!

- Explain that rhyming words sound the same at the end. "Blow" and "go"; "corn" and "morn"; "bake" and "make"; "too" and "goo" are all rhyming word pairs. Try pausing just before the end of a rhyming pair and encourage the children to supply the rhyming word (such as "make" and "goo" above) with the support of visual clues or context, or simply through the sounds suggested by the rhyme.

- Blend word parts in a variety of ways.

  Syllables: wind ... mill. What's the word? (*Windmill.*)

  Onset sound: /g/ ... o. What's the word? (*Go.*) What other words start with /g/?

  Phoneme by phoneme (for older children, in primary grades): /m/-/i/-/ll/. What's the word? (*Mill.*)

- Practice segmenting or "stretching" the nursery rhyme words (for older children, in primary grades). Show the children a rubber band and stretch it out and in. As you stretch the rubber band out longer, you can see all of its parts more clearly. Explain that

you can also stretch words, so that you can hear each individual sound (phoneme) in the word. Stretch the word "go": /g/-/o/. Sometimes one phoneme is represented by more than one letter, such as in the word "mill": /m/-/i/-/ll/. "Mill" contains three phonemes. Stretch other nursery rhyme words.

- Clap words: Clap once for each word in the rhyme, following the poster. Introduce variety by stomping feet or jumping once for each word.

- Clap syllables: Older children can learn to clap once for each syllable in the rhyme. Practice with one word at a time as the children begin to understand the concept. For example: Blow (1 clap); wind (1 clap); blow (1 clap); And (1 clap); go (1 clap); mill (1 clap); go (1 clap); That (1 clap); the (1 clap); mil-ler (2 claps); may (1 clap); grind (1 clap); his (1 clap); corn (1 clap). Introduce variety by stomping feet or jumping to the syllables.

Print Awareness (*Notice print and know how to handle books and follow the written word on a page.*)

- Point to the "Blow, Wind, Blow!" poster. Say: "Our nursery rhyme is written right up here. I'll read it aloud, and then we'll say it again together." Follow the text of the rhyme with your finger as you read the poster, from left to right.

- Occasionally turn the poster upside down or sideways and see if the children detect the problem.

Narrative Skills (*Practice retelling stories or events, sequencing the order in which events happened, and adding descriptions.*)

- Talk and ask two or three open-ended questions about the rhyme and the objects and characters in it, and allow the children to ask questions. Avoid asking yes/no questions unless there is a specific purpose in doing so. Qualify questions by including the phrase "do you think," as in "Why do you think ...?" or "What do you think ...?" This type of question does not have a "right" answer that children are afraid they will get wrong. For example: What do you think the

miller will do with the flour after he grinds it from the corn? What do you think the baker will do with the flour? What might the baker do with the bread that she bakes? With whom do you think the baker will share the bread she bakes? What else might the baker make with the leftover flour? Have you ever helped make anything with flour?

- If you have a small enough group and adequate time, act out "Blow, Wind, Blow!" with creative dramatics. Have one group of children be the windmill, another group be millers, a third group be bakers, and the last group be the bread. Make sure that each child gets to play all of the different roles if possible, and to choose who or what they want to be.

Letter Knowledge—Letter W (*Learn to recognize and identify letters, knowing that they have different names and sounds and that the same letter can look different.*)

- Show a large size cutout or magnet-backed foam letter "W" and "w" (see Resources). Point to the capital "W" letter that begins the word "Wind" in the title of your poster. Say: "Here is the letter W—a big uppercase, or capital W." Draw the capital letter "W" in the air as a group. Point to a small letter "w" on the poster within the rhyme's text. Say: "Here is also the letter w—a small, lowercase w." Draw a lowercase "w" in the air as a group. Make the /W/ sound and say: "W is for Wind; W is for Water; W is for Wish; W is for Window; W is for Wait; W is for Worm; W is for Wash; W is for Want." Encourage the audience to repeat each phrase after you. Include three or four examples.

- Demonstrate making the shapes of "W" and "w" using string or pipe cleaners.

Parent/Caregiver Connection

- Reinforce the parent/caregiver's key role in their child's early literacy development through comfortable, relaxed times together with songs, rhymes, and books. Emphasize fun and enjoyment as the goals.

- Encourage caregivers to participate during storytime and to incorporate "Blow, Wind, Blow!" at home during play and reading

times. Select one of the "Blow, Wind, Blow!" early literacy activities that you share together during storytime, and briefly explain how the activity supports children's early literacy development. Suggest repeating the activity at home. Try different activities to highlight different skills during each storytime.

- Share information about Dialogic, or "Hear and Say" Reading (see Resources). Encourage parents and caregivers to individually discuss the day's rhyme, its characters, and events in an open-ended way with their children, following the child's interest while affirming and expanding upon their answers. For example, point to the windmill in "Blow, Wind, Blow!" and ask, "What is this?" Child: "Windmill." Follow up with positive affirmation, and enlarge: "Yes, it's a windmill. What does it do?" Child: "Go." Expand: "Yes, the windmill can go around and around when the wind blows." Help the child repeat longer phrases. Ask open-ended questions such as: "What do you see in this picture?" Build on the things that catch the child's interest. This type of positive, interactive discussion around familiar rhymes and books helps improve early language development, communication, and parent/child relationships.

Take-home "Blow, Wind, Blow!"

Copy the "Blow, Wind, Blow!" illustrations from page 30 onto card stock and distribute. Color, cut out, and assemble the pieces at the end of storytime, or encourage the families to do so at home. Affix the windmill's arms to the windmill with a metal brad fastener or knotted yarn. Make a sample of the take-home version and demonstrate singing or saying the rhyme using the small pieces. (Families may affix sticky-back magnet material to pieces for playtime use on a magnetic surface such as a cookie sheet or the refrigerator if desired. Be aware of choking hazard considerations for younger children.)

Additional Extension Ideas

Note: For all craft activities, provide materials for adult attendees as well as children. Encourage children and adults to talk together about what they are making, and to use the completed crafts to retell or act out the rhyme.

- Show the pictures from several different nursery rhyme books that illustrate "Blow, Wind, Blow!" and repeat the rhyme together with each new illustration. Talk about the differences between the various illustrations.

- Make pinwheels and blow them as you say "Blow, Wind, Blow!"

- Talk about: What else does the wind do besides turning a windmill's arms to grind grain? *(Fly kites, dry clothes on the clothesline, blow sailboats, generate wind energy, etc.)*

- Read *The Wind Blew* by Pat Hutchins (Macmillan, 1974). Rhyming text describes the antics of a capricious wind.

- Make a Huffing and Puffing Mr. Wind Puppet. Complete instructions are included in *Crafts to Make in the Spring* by Kathy Ross (Millbrook Press, 1998).

- If you have your group for an extended time period, make bread in a bread machine. Dump in the ingredients as a group, and turn the machine on. If you don't have enough time for the bread to bake, prepare a loaf ahead of time so you can see and taste the finished product.

- Show real samples of various kinds of bread, including breads from around the world. Wheat bread, white bread, pita bread, naan, tortillas, biscuits, breadsticks, pumpernickel and rye bread, and so forth.

- Read *Peanut Butter & Jelly: A Play Rhyme* illustrated by Nadine Bernard Westcott (Dutton Children's Books, 1993, 1987). Rhyming text and illustrations explain how to make a peanut butter and jelly sandwich.

  Share the "Peanut Butter and Jelly" action rhyme as a group.

  Refrain:
  Peanut *(Clap)* butter, *(Slap knees.)*
  Peanut *(Clap)* butter, *(Slap knees.)*
  Jelly, *(Clap, slap knees.)*
  Jelly. *(Clap, slap knees.)*

First you take the dough and knead it, knead it. *(Push with heels of hands.)*

Refrain

Pop it in the oven and bake it, bake it. *(Extend arms towards "oven.")*

Refrain

Then you take a knife and slice it, slice it. *("Saw" back and forth with the side of your hand.)*

Refrain

Then you take the peanuts and crack them, crack them. *(Pound fists together.)*

Refrain

Put them on the floor and mash them, mash them. *(Push fist into palm of other hand.)*

Refrain

Then you take a knife and spread it, spread it. *(Move hand back and forth as if spreading the peanut butter.)*

Refrain

Next you take some grapes and squash them, squash them. *(Stamp feet.)*

Refrain

Glop it on the bread and smear it, smear it. *(Spreading motion again.)*

Refrain

Then you take the sandwich and eat it, eat it. *(Open and close mouth as if biting a sandwich.)*

Refrain

- Read *The Giant Jam Sandwich* by John Vernon Lord, with verses by Janet Burroway (Houghton Mifflin, 1973, 1972). When four million wasps fly into Itching Down, the village's residents devise a clever way to get rid of them.

- Make a giant classroom craft sandwich with poster board or thick foam bread. Paint brown "peanut butter" onto the bread and allow the paint to dry completely. Add some red or purple painted "jelly" and allow to dry, then glue on additional felt, foamies, or paper sandwich items.

- Paint individual giant craft sandwiches.

- Make individual small-size "sandwiches" crafts. Cut out doubled, bread-slice shaped card stock or construction paper pieces, leaving a "hinge" of paper along one side so that the sandwich will open and close like a card. Decorate with crayons or markers and felt, paper, tissue paper, and foamies sandwich fillings.

- Explain how a mill worked historically. The wind's power (or the power of running water) turned stone "buhrs" that ground the grain into flour. Millstones consisted of a bottom bed stone in a fixed position and a revolving upper stone, with corrugations (alternating ridges or grooves) on each of the opposing surfaces.

- Make the shapes of "W" and "w" using string, pipe cleaners, or clay.

Blow, Wind, Blow!

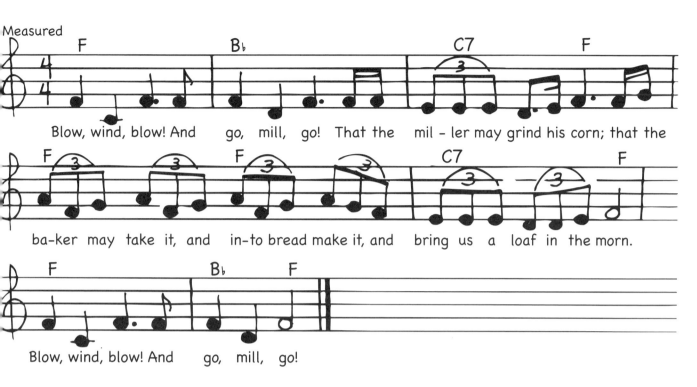

Blow, wind, blow! And go, mill, go! That the mil - ler may grind his corn; that the

ba-ker may take it, and in-to bread make it, and bring us a loaf in the morn.

Blow, wind, blow! And go, mill, go!

Take-home Blow, Wind, Blow

Blow, wind, blow!

And go, mill, go!

That the miller may grind his corn;

That the baker may take it,

And into bread make it,

And bring us a loaf in the morn.

Blow, wind, blow!

And go, mill go!

Chook, Chook, Chook

> "Chook chook, chook chook chook,
>
> Good morning, Mrs. Hen.
>
> How many children have you got?"
>
> "Madam, I have ten:
>
> Four of them are yellow,
>
> And four of them are brown,
>
> And two of them are speckled red,
>
> The nicest in the town."

Variants

Originally "Chuck, chuck, chuck, chuck," the rhyme also referred to "pretty hen" instead of "Mrs. Hen." At that time (1866) three of the chickens were yellow, three were brown, and "four of them [were] black-and-white." The black-and-white chickens later became "black and brown," and in more recent versions of the rhyme they are "speckled red" as they are here. The original asks: "How many chickens have you got?"

A wonderful bouncing and counting rhyme, "Chook, Chook, Chook" also adapts beautifully to the tune of "The Grand Old Duke of York."

History

Apparently written by "Uncle James" especially for the inaugural issue of *The Infant's Magazine* (Vol. 1, No. 1, January 1866), the rhyme has been repeated and adapted over the years.

Musical Notation

See musical notation on page 36.

Preparing and Using the Mother Goose Rhyme Time Pieces

"Chook, Chook, Chook" pieces:

- Mother Hen
- Four yellow chicks in a group
- Four brown chicks in a group
- Two speckled red chicks in a group
- "Chook, Chook, Chook" poster

Organize the "Chook, Chook, Chook" rhyme pieces ahead of time in the order in which they appear in the rhyme: the two speckled red chicks on the bottom of the stack, the four brown chicks on top of them, the four yellow chicks on top of the brown chicks, and the mother hen on the very top. Hide the stack out of sight.

Before sharing the rhyme, place the poster on an easel so the audience can see it clearly. Hold Mother Hen in one hand as you sing the rhyme. With your other hand, hold up each set of baby chicks and then put them down again as you sing, or affix the pieces to a large Velcro or magnet board. If you wish to incorporate motions or use a musical instrument for accompaniment, point to each piece on the board in turn as you lead the group in the actions or play and sing the song.

Utilize the sections of Mother Goose Rhyme Time that work best for you and your storytime group or classroom. Experiment with new ideas and techniques. Practice ahead of time so you feel comfortable with the material and can focus on the audience rather than on trying to remember how you intended to share the rhyme.

Storytime

Share "Chook Chook Chook" as a song or as a chant; bouncing, patting your lap, clapping, or jumping to keep a rhythm. Sing or say the rhyme quickly and slowly, loudly and quietly. Incorporate movements as desired.

Babies (*Sitting on caregivers' laps*)

"Chook chook, chook chook chook,
(*Clap hands and/or bounce baby.*)
Good morning, Mrs. Hen.
(*Wave enthusiastically.*)
How many children have you got?"
(*Hold out hands questioningly.*)
"Madam, I have ten:
(*Hold up ten fingers.*)
Four of them are yellow,
(*Hold up four fingers on one hand.*)
And four of them are brown,
(*Hold up four fingers on the other hand.*)
And two of them are speckled red,
(*Hold up two fingers on the first hand.*)
The nicest in the town."
(*Clap hands and/or bounce baby.*)

Older Children (*Standing or sitting*)

"Chook chook, chook chook chook,
(*Clap hands, pat lap, or jump rhythmically.*)
Good morning, Mrs. Hen.
(*Wave enthusiastically.*)
How many children have you got?"
(*Hold out hands questioningly.*)

"Madam, I have ten:
(*Hold up ten fingers.*)
Four of them are yellow,
(*Hold up four fingers on one hand.*)
And four of them are brown,
(*Hold up four fingers on the other hand.*)
And two of them are speckled red,
(*Hold up two fingers on the first hand.*)
The nicest in the town."
(*Clap hands, pat lap, or jump rhythmically.*)

Early Literacy Activities

Consider integrating several of the activities or techniques suggested below as you share the nursery rhyme. All activities should be approached in a fun and playful manner, encouraging curiosity and allowing for children's individual differences. **Note:** Be aware of children's developmental stages and focus on the activities that are appropriate for the ages and stages of your group. The suggestions provided are intended to give you a variety of ideas to work with over time. You will not incorporate all of the techniques at once. Share one rhyme several times during a single storytime, and repeat the same rhyme over several storytimes. Try different activities to highlight a different skill during each storytime.

Print Motivation (*Encourage interest in and excitement about reading and books.*)

* Say the words rhythmically and with enthusiasm, conveying your enjoyment of the rhyme.

* Create a clucking voice for Mrs. Hen, and change your tone and facial expression as appropriate to the context.

* Repeat the rhyme several times together with the children, encouraging their own enjoyment and internalization of its lively rhythms.

Language and Vocabulary (*Introduce and explain new words or new meanings to familiar words.*)

* Use the rhyme pieces to illustrate and help explain language and vocabulary. Say: "'Chook' is another way of saying 'cluck.' Who says 'cluck'? Chickens. Perhaps we're introducing ourselves to Mrs. Hen (*point to*

hen) in chicken language! A hen is a grown-up girl chicken, and a rooster is a grown-up boy chicken. Mrs. Hen has ten children! Four of her baby chicks are the color yellow *(point to the yellow chicks and count them)*, and four of them are brown *(point to the brown chicks and count them)*, and two of them are speckled red *(point to the speckled red chicks and count them)*. A speckle is a little spot, and speckled means covered all over with lots of little spots. The baby chicks are the nicest in the town."

- Talk or sing about the illustrations: "I see a mother hen." "I see four baby chicks." Pause for the children to name the object to which you are pointing: "I see a _____." Expand on descriptive features of the illustrations to build vocabulary and encourage the children's awareness of and attention to details: "I see some baby chicks. Four yellow baby chicks."

Phonological Awareness *(Play with rhymes, practice breaking words apart and putting them back together, and listen for beginning sounds and alliteration.)*

- Explain that rhyming words sound the same at the end. "Hen" and "ten" are rhyming word pairs, as are "brown" and "town." Try pausing just before the end of a rhyming pair and encourage the children to supply the rhyming word with the support of visual clues or context, or simply through the sounds suggested by the rhyme.

- Play an "oddity task" game. For example, which word does not rhyme? Them, brown, town. *(Answer: them.)* Which word sounds different at the beginning? Hen, red, how. *(Answer: red.)* Which word sounds different at the end? Hen, brown, four. *(Answer: four.)*

- Blend word parts in a variety of ways.

  Syllables: yel ... low. What's the word? *(Yellow.)*

  Onset sound: /t/ ... own. What's the word? *(Town.)* What other words start with /t/?

  Phoneme by phoneme (for older children, in primary grades): /r/-/e/-/d/. What's the word? *(Red.)*

- Practice segmenting or "stretching" the nursery rhyme words (for older children, in primary grades). Show the children a rubber band and stretch it out and in. As you stretch the rubber band out longer, you can see all of its parts more clearly. Explain that you can also stretch words, so that you can hear each individual sound (phoneme) in the word. Stretch the word "hen": /h/-/e/-/n/. Sometimes one phoneme is represented by more than one letter, such as in the word "chook": /ch/-/oo/-/k/. "Chook" contains three phonemes. Stretch other nursery rhyme words.

- Clap words: Clap once for each word in the rhyme, following the poster. Introduce variety by stomping feet or jumping once for each word.

- Clap syllables: Older children can learn to clap once for each syllable in the rhyme. Practice with one word at a time as the children begin to understand the concept. For example: Chook (1 clap); chook (1 clap); chook (1 clap); chook (1 clap); chook (1 clap); Good (1 clap); morn-ing (2 claps); Mrs. (2 claps); Hen (1 clap). Introduce variety by stomping feet or jumping to the syllables.

Print Awareness *(Notice print and know how to handle books and follow the written word on a page.)*

- Point to the "Chook, Chook, Chook" poster. Say: "Our nursery rhyme is written right up here. I'll read it aloud, and then we'll say it again together." Follow the text of the rhyme with your finger as you read the poster, from left to right.

- Occasionally turn the poster upside down or sideways and see if the children detect the problem.

Narrative Skills *(Practice retelling stories or events, sequencing the order in which events happened, and adding descriptions.)*

- Talk and ask two or three open-ended questions about the rhyme and the characters in it, and allow the children to ask questions. Avoid asking yes/no questions unless there is a specific purpose in doing so. Qualify questions by including the phrase

"do you think," as in "Why do you think ...?" or "What do you think ...?" This type of question does not have a "right" answer that children are afraid they will get wrong. For example: What kinds of things do you think Mrs. Hen and her children do all day? They probably scratch around for food, but do you think they play games, too? If so, what kind of games? Where do you think they might go to play? Is there a chicken park they can visit? What do you think the chicken children's names might be?

- If you have a small enough group and adequate time, act out "Chook, Chook, Chook" with creative dramatics and counting. Pretend to be Mrs. Hen, and have the children order themselves in three variable sized rows of baby chicks. Count the numbers of chicken children in each group together, then all say the rhyme using those numbers.

Letter Knowledge—Letter M (*Learn to recognize and identify letters, knowing that they have different names and sounds and that the same letter can look different.*)

- Show a large-size cutout or magnet-backed foam letter "M" and "m" (see Resources). Point to the capital "M" letters that begin the words "Mrs." and "Madam" in the text of your poster. Say: "Here is the letter M—a big uppercase, or capital M." Draw the capital letter "M" in the air as a group. Point to a small letter "m" on the poster within the rhyme's text. Say: "Here is also the letter m—a small, lowercase m." Draw a lowercase "m" in the air as a group. Make the /M/ sound and say: "M is for Mrs.; M is for Madam; M is for Moon; M is for Mouse; M is for Milk; M is for Mail; M is for Mommy; M is for Man; M is for Me." Encourage the audience to repeat each phrase after you. Include three or four examples.

- Demonstrate making the shapes of "M" and "m" using string or pipe cleaners.

Parent/Caregiver Connection

- Reinforce the parent/caregiver's key role in their child's early literacy development through comfortable, relaxed times together with songs, rhymes, and books. Emphasize fun and enjoyment as the goals.

- Encourage caregivers to participate during storytime and to incorporate "Chook, Chook, Chook" at home during play and reading times. Select one of the "Chook, Chook, Chook" early literacy activities that you share together during storytime, and briefly explain how the activity supports children's early literacy development. Suggest repeating the activity at home. Try different activities to highlight different skills during each storytime.

- Share information about Dialogic, or "Hear and Say" Reading (see Resources). Encourage parents and caregivers to individually discuss the day's rhyme, its characters, and events in an open-ended way with their children, following the child's interest while affirming and expanding upon their answers. For example, point to Mrs. Hen in "Chook, Chook, Chook" and ask, "Who is this?" Child: "Mommy." Follow up with positive affirmation, and enlarge: "Yes, it's the mommy hen, named Mrs. Hen. What do you see when you look at her picture?" Child: "The tail." Expand: "Yes, she has a big brown tail with four feathers." Help the child repeat longer phrases. Ask open-ended questions such as: "What do you see in this picture?" Build on the things that catch the child's interest. This type of positive, interactive discussion around familiar rhymes and books helps improve early language development, communication, and parent/child relationships.

Take-home "Chook, Chook, Chook"

Copy the "Chook, Chook, Chook" illustrations from pages 37–38 onto card stock and distribute. Color and cut out the pieces at the end of storytime, or encourage the families to do so at home. Make a sample of the take-home version, and demonstrate singing or saying the rhyme using the small pieces. (Families may affix sticky-back magnet material to pieces for playtime use on a magnetic surface such as a cookie sheet or the refrigerator if desired. Be aware of choking hazard considerations for younger children.)

Additional Extension Ideas

Note: For all craft activities, provide materials for adult attendees as well as children. Encourage children and adults to talk together about what they are making, and to use the completed crafts to retell or act out the rhyme.

- Show the pictures from several different nursery rhyme books that illustrate "Chook, Chook, Chook" and repeat the rhyme together with each new illustration. Talk about the differences between the various illustrations.

- Make baby chicks for Mrs. Hen. Cut out baby chick shapes from card stock or construction paper and distribute to the children to decorate as desired. Provide colored craft feathers, google eyes, felt, foamies, tacky glue, glitter, crayons, markers, and so forth. Use a hen puppet or the Mrs. Hen rhyme piece to comment approvingly in a chicken voice on the lovely chicken children as they are being made.

- Make hatching eggs. Cut out large elongated egg shapes from white or light brown card stock. Cut the eggs in half from side to side and place them together again, slightly overlapping the straight center edge. Make a small slit at one of the overlapping corners, through both layers of the egg. Insert a metal brad fastener into the slit (or double-knot a piece of yarn through it) so the egg swivels open and closed. Decorate the top half of a chick and glue it behind the bottom half of the egg with the chick sticking out. When you open the egg, the baby chick appears. Decorate eggs as desired to match the baby chicks.

- Make baby chicks with round egg-shaped bodies, attaching flappable wings to their sides with metal brad fasteners or knotted yarn. Give each chick google eyes and a foamies beak, or draw them on. Glue on orange feet that stick out below the body.

- Adapt a Little White Duck craft as a Baby Chick simply by changing the shape of the bird's construction paper feet. The bird's body is made from the outline of the child's foot, and the two wings are made from tracings of the child's two hands. Adapt the colors to match the yellow, brown, and speckled red chicks in "Chook, Chook, Chook," or allow the children to creatively select a color. See Little White Duck in *Crafts to Make in the Spring* by Kathy Ross (Millbrook Press, 1998).

- Read *Charlie the Chicken: A Pop-up Book* by Nick Denchfield (Red Wagon Books, 1997). Charlie the chicken eats lots of healthy food so he will grow big and strong.

- Change the number and color of the baby chicks in the rhyme and repeat. Make sets of differently colored chickens to illustrate.

- Math sets: Cut out variously colored and sized individual baby chicks (or colored circles to represent the chicks). Group the chicks into sets by color, size, number of beaks (all have one beak), and so forth.

- Play an egg-hatching memory game. Cut out sets of egg shapes from card stock and glue various colors or numbers of baby chicks to the back of the eggs. Children try and remember where the matching chicks are concealed, following classic "memory game" rules.

- Read *Mrs. Hen's Big Surprise* by Christel Desmoinaux (Margaret K. McElderry Books, 2000). When Mrs. Hen discovers a very large, strange-looking egg in her garden, she is sure it will hatch into the baby chick of her dreams. Her patience is rewarded when the egg hatches at last, although she is in for a bit of a surprise when her new baby turns out to be a dinosaur!

- Make the shapes of "M" and "m" using string, pipe cleaners, or clay.

Chook, Chook, Chook

Triumphantly

G   A7

"Chook chook, chook chook chook, good   morn-ing Mrs. — Hen. How

D7   D7   G

man - y chil-dren have you got?" "Ma — I have ten:

dam3

G   A7

four of them are yel — low, and four of them are brown, and

D7   D7   G

two of them are speck-led red, the nic - est in the town."

Take-home Chook, Chook, Chook

"Chook chook, chook chook chook,

Good morning, Mrs. Hen.

How many children have you got?"

"Madam, I have ten:

Four of them are yellow,

And four of them are brown,

And two of them are speckled red,

The nicest in the town."

Dickery Dickery Dare

> Dickery dickery dare,
>
> The pig flew up in the air!
>
> The man in brown
>
> Soon brought him down,
>
> Dickery dickery dare.

Variants

Recent versions of this rhyme are remarkably standard, with few variations. The earliest version, however, reads "Clickety, clickety clare, The pig he flew in the air, The man in brown, soon fetch'd him down, Clickety Clickety clare." The rhyme is frequently sung to the same tune as "Hickory Dickory Dock" and/or "Higglety, Pigglety, Pop!"

History

The first documented appearance of the rhyme was in the *Second Royal Infant Opera* by O. B. Dussek in 1842.

Musical Notation

See musical notation on page 44.

Preparing and Using the Mother Goose Rhyme Time Pieces

"Dickery Dickery Dare" pieces:

- Large pig

- Man in brown

- "Dickery Dickery Dare" poster

Before sharing the rhyme, place the poster on an easel so the audience can see it clearly. Hold the pig in one hand as you say the rhyme, quickly lifting it high as you reach "up in the air." With your other hand, raise the man in brown next to the pig and lower both figures back down as you say "brought him down."

You can incorporate actions for the rhyme while holding the rhyme pieces, bouncing the pig and lifting him up or jumping with him, and bringing him down again. If you wish to use a musical instrument for accompaniment or prefer to have your hands free while leading the group in the motions, however, affix the pieces to a large Velcro or magnet board. Point to each piece on the board as you lead the group in the actions or play and sing the song.

Utilize the sections of Mother Goose Rhyme Time that work best for you and your storytime group or classroom. Experiment with new ideas and techniques. Practice ahead of time so you feel comfortable with the material and can focus on the audience rather than on trying to remember how you intended to share the rhyme.

Storytime

Share "Dickery Dickery Dare" as a song or as a chant; bouncing, patting your lap, or clapping to keep a rhythm. Sing or say the rhyme quickly and slowly, loudly and quietly. Incorporate movements and animal noises as desired. Encourage the children's caregivers to adapt motions or make up new ones as appropriate for their child; many different actions are possible. Here are a few options:

Babies (*Sitting on caregivers' laps*)

> Dickery dickery dare,
> (*Bounce baby.*)
> The pig flew up in the air!
> (*Lift baby UP.*)
> The man in brown
> Soon brought him down,
> (*Lower baby to your lap again.*)
> Dickery dickery dare.
> (*Bounce baby.*)

Older Children (*Sitting or standing*)

> Dickery dickery dare,
> (*Clap or pat lap rhythmically.*)
> The pig flew up in the air!
> (*Raise arms overhead or jump high.*)
> The man in brown
> Soon brought him down,
> (*Bring arms down low or crouch low.*)
> Dickery dickery dare.
> (*Clap hands or pat lap rhythmically.*)

Early Literacy Activities

Consider integrating one or several of the activities or techniques suggested below as you share the nursery rhyme. All activities should be approached in a fun and playful manner, encouraging curiosity and allowing for children's individual differences. **Note:** Be aware of children's developmental stages and focus on the activities that are appropriate for the ages and stages of your group. The suggestions provided are intended to give you a variety of ideas to work with over time. You will not incorporate all of the techniques at once. Share one rhyme several times during a single storytime, and repeat the same rhyme over several storytimes. Try different activities to highlight a different skill during each storytime.

Print Motivation (*Encourage interest in and excitement about reading and books.*)

- Say the words rhythmically and with enthusiasm, conveying your enjoyment of the rhyme.

- Repeat the rhyme several times together with the children, encouraging their own enjoyment and internalization of its lively rhythms.

Language and Vocabulary (*Introduce and explain new words or new meanings to familiar words.*)

- Use the rhyme pieces to illustrate and help explain language and vocabulary. Say: "'Dickery Dickery Dare' are nonsense words that introduce us to the rest of our nursery rhyme. The pig (*point to the pig*) flew up in the air (*lift the pig up high*). When we say the pig flew up, it just means that he went up quickly—not that he flew like a bird. The man (*point to the man*) in brown is called that because he is wearing brown clothes. The man brought the pig back down (*move the pig from up high down to a lower vantage*) again so he was back where he started."

- Talk or sing about the illustrations: "I see a man." "I see a pig." Pause for the children to name the object to which you are pointing: "I see a _____." Expand on descriptive features of the illustrations to build vocabulary and encourage the children's awareness of and attention to details: "I see a man. A man wearing brown clothes and a brown hat."

Phonological Awareness (*Play with rhymes, practice breaking words apart and putting them back together, and listen for beginning sounds and alliteration.*)

- Play with the words, animals, and colors in the rhyme and change them. Use puppets or props to dramatize. For example:

> Dickery dickery dare,
> The cow flew up in the air!
> The man in black
> Soon brought her back,
> Dickery dickery dare.

Dickery dickery dare,
The cat flew up in the air!
The boy in blue
Flew up there too,
Dickery dickery dare.

Dickery dickery dare
The dog flew up in the air!
The girl in white
Said, "What a sight!"
Dickery dickery dare!

- Explain that rhyming words sound the same at the end. "Dare" and "air"; "brown" and "down"; "black" and "back"; "blue" and "too"; "white" and "sight" are all rhyming word pairs. Try pausing just before the end of a rhyming pair and encourage the children to supply the rhyming word (such as "back," "too," and "sight" above) with the support of visual clues or context, or simply through the sounds suggested by the rhyme.

- Play an "oddity task" game. For example, which word does not rhyme? Dare, flew, air. *(Answer: flew.)* Which word sounds different at the beginning? Dickery, down, pig. *(Answer: pig.)* Which word sounds different at the end? Up, man, brown. *(Answer: up.)*

- Blend word parts in a variety of ways.

  Syllables: Pig ... pen. What's the word? *(Pigpen.)*

  Onset sound: /p/ ... ig. What's the word? *(Pig.)* What other words start with /p/?

  Phoneme by phoneme (for older children, in primary grades): /m/-/a/-/n/. What's the word? *(Man.)*

- Practice segmenting or "stretching" the nursery rhyme words (for older children, in primary grades). Show the children a rubber band and stretch it out and in. As you stretch the rubber band out longer, you can see all of its parts more clearly. Explain that you can also stretch words, so that you can hear each individual sound (phoneme) in the word. Stretch the word "pig": /p/-/i/-/g/. Sometimes one phoneme is represented by more than one letter, such as in the word "soon": /s/-/oo/-/n/. "Soon"

contains three phonemes. Stretch other nursery rhyme words.

- Clap words: Clap once for each word in the rhyme, following the poster. Introduce variety by stomping feet or jumping once for each word.

- Clap syllables: Older children can learn to clap once for each syllable in the rhyme. Practice with one word at a time as the children begin to understand the concept. For example: Dick-er-y (3 claps); dick-er-y (3 claps); dare (1 clap); The (1 clap); pig (1 clap); flew (1 clap); up (1 clap); in (1 clap); the (1 clap); air (1 clap). Introduce variety by stomping feet or jumping to the syllables.

Print Awareness (*Notice print and know how to handle books and follow the written word on a page.*)

- Point to the "Dickery Dickery Dare" poster. Say: "Our nursery rhyme is written right up here. I'll read it aloud, and then we'll say it again together." Follow the text of the rhyme with your finger as you read the poster, from left to right.

- Occasionally turn the poster upside down or sideways and see if the children detect the problem.

Narrative Skills (*Practice retelling stories or events, sequencing the order in which events happened, and adding descriptions.*)

- Talk and ask two or three open-ended questions about the rhyme and the objects and characters in it, and allow the children to ask questions. Avoid asking yes/no questions unless there is a specific purpose in doing so. Qualify questions by including the phrase "do you think," as in "Why do you think ...?" or "What do you think ...?" This type of question does not have a "right" answer that children are afraid they will get wrong. For example: What do you think might have happened to the pig that made him fly up in the air? Who do you think the man in brown might be? Why do you think the man was wearing brown clothes? How do you think the man in brown managed to get the pig back down again? What do you think the man and the pig did after they got back down?

- Act out "Dickery Dickery Dare" as a group with creative dramatics, using your paper plate pigs and wearing your brown paper bag vests and hats (see Additional Extension Ideas below). Repeat the rhyme with: "The girls in brown / Soon brought him down" and "The boys in brown / Soon brought him down."

Letter Knowledge—Letter D (*Learn to recognize and identify letters, knowing that they have different names and sounds and that the same letter can look different.*)

- Show a large size cutout or magnet-backed foam letter "D" and "d" (see Resources). Point to the capital "D" letters that begin the words "Dickery, Dickery, and Dare" in the title of your poster. Say: "Here is the letter D—a big uppercase, or capital D." Draw the capital letter "D" in the air as a group. Point to a small letter "d" on the poster within the rhyme's text. Say: "Here is also the letter d—a small, lowercase d." Draw a lowercase "d" in the air as a group. Make the /D/ sound and say: "D is for Dickery Dickery; D is for Dare; D is for Duck; D is for Dinosaur; D is for Dog; D is for Dance; D is for Doll; D is for Door; D is for Doughnut; D is for Daddy." Encourage the audience to repeat each phrase after you. Include three or four examples.

- Demonstrate making the shapes of "D" and "d" using string or pipe cleaners.

Parent/Caregiver Connection

- Reinforce the parent/caregiver's key role in their child's early literacy development through comfortable, relaxed times together with songs, rhymes, and books. Emphasize fun and enjoyment as the goals.

- Encourage caregivers to participate during storytime and incorporate "Dickery Dickery Dare" at home during play and reading times. Select one of the "Dickery Dickery Dare" early literacy activities that you share together during storytime, and briefly explain how the activity supports children's early literacy development. Suggest repeat-

ing the activity at home. Try different activities to highlight different skills during each storytime.

- Share information about Dialogic, or "Hear and Say" Reading (see Resources). Encourage parents and caregivers to individually discuss the day's rhyme, its characters, and events in an open-ended way with their children, following the child's interest while affirming and expanding upon their answers. For example, point to the man in "Dickery Dickery Dare" and ask, "Who is this?" Child: "A man." Follow up with positive affirmation, and enlarge: "Yes, it's a man dressed in brown clothes and a brown hat. What do you see when you look at his picture?" Child: "Hand." Expand: "Yes, the man is reaching up in the air with his hand." Help the child repeat longer phrases. Ask open-ended questions such as: "What do you see in this picture?" Build on the things that catch the child's interest. This type of positive, interactive discussion around familiar rhymes and books helps improve early language development, communication, and parent/child relationships.

Take-home "Dickery Dickery Dare"

Copy the "Dickery Dickery Dare" illustrations from pages 45–46 onto card stock and distribute. Color and cut out the pieces at the end of storytime, or encourage the families to do so at home. Make a sample of the take-home version, and demonstrate singing or saying the rhyme using the small pieces. (Families may affix sticky-back magnet material to pieces for playtime use on a magnetic surface such as a cookie sheet or the refrigerator if desired. Be aware of choking hazard considerations for younger children.)

Additional Extension Ideas

Note: For all craft activities, provide materials for adult attendees as well as children. Encourage children and adults to talk together about what they are making, and to use the completed crafts to retell or act out the rhyme.

- Show the pictures from several different nursery rhyme books that illustrate "Dickery

Dickery Dare" and repeat the rhyme together with each new illustration. Talk about the differences between the various illustrations.

• Make "boy in brown" and "girl in brown" paper grocery bag vests and hats. To make a vest, turn a standard-sized grocery bag upside down so the open end is at the bottom. Cut the bag from bottom to top along the center front. Continue cutting a neck hole from the solid bottom of the bag. Cut armholes in the sides of the bag. Decorate the vest by fringing it with scissors and/or with brown paint, crayons, stickers, foamies, felt, and so forth. Make paper grocery bag hats from slightly smaller, thinner brown paper bags. To determine hat size, turn the bag upside down above the child's head, so that it is positioned above the child's ears. Fold over the excess paper bag (like wrapping your pants around your leg to slide into a pair of tall boots) and hold the bag in place, lifting it back up and off the child's head. Begin rolling the paper bag out and down on itself a number of times to form a somewhat bunchy rolled hatband with the rest of the paper bag forming the hat's crown. Decorate the hat as desired with brown paint, crayons, stickers, foamies, felt, and so forth.

• Make "Dickery Dickery Dare" paper plate pigs. Sponge paint standard-sized paper plates using pink paint. The plates will be the pigs' bodies. Cut out pink construction paper heads, feet, ears, and snouts. Glue to the pig bodies. Using crayons, markers, paint, or colored pencils, decorate with eyes, mouths, nostrils, hooves, and brown "mud" as desired. Paper punch a small hole at the side of the plate (serving as the pig's back end) through which the children can twist a pink pipe cleaner tail. Wrap the tails around a crayon, pencil, or your finger to curl.

• Make the shapes of "D" and "d" using string, pipe cleaners, or clay.

Dickery Dickery Dare

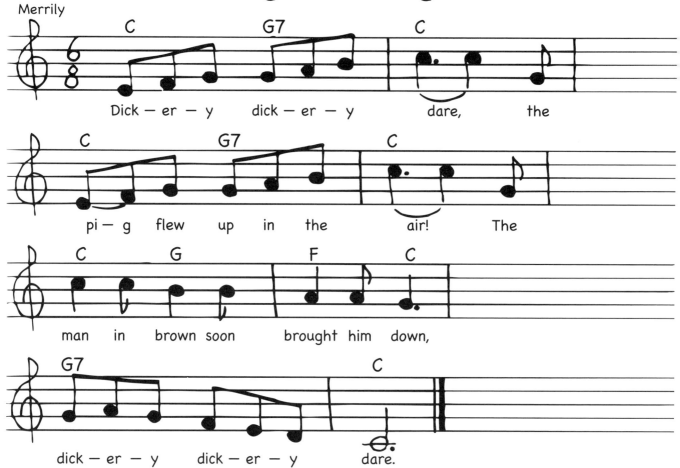

Merrily

C   G7   C

Dick — er — y   dick — er — y   dare,   the

C   G7   C

pi — g   flew   up   in   the   air!   The

C   G   F   C

man   in   brown soon   brought him   down,

G7   C

dick — er — y   dick — er — y   dare.

Take-home Dickery Dickery Dare

Dickery dickery dare,

The pig flew up in the air!

The man in brown

Soon brought him down,

Dickery dickery dare.

Hickety Pickety

> Hickety Pickety, my black hen,
>
> She lays eggs for women and men.
>
> Sometimes ONE,
>
> And sometimes TEN!
>
> Hickety Pickety, my black hen.

Variants

Some versions replace "Hickety Pickety" with "Higgledy Piggledy," and the hen usually only "lays eggs for gentlemen." Hickety Pickety is sometimes referred to as "my little hen" instead of "my black hen." Before detailing the quantity of eggs, the rhyme often reads: "Gentlemen come every day / To see what my black hen doth lay." Typically the numbers are "Sometimes nine and sometimes ten."

History

The rhyme is possibly a more wholesome descendant of an older verse about "Little Blue Betty" from the early 1800s. Appearing in its modern guise in 1853, "Hickety Pickety" has been incorporated into various games ("Ticky, ticky, touchwood, my black hen") and activities throughout the years.

Musical Notation

See musical notation on page 52.

Preparing and Using the Mother Goose Rhyme Time Pieces

"Hickety Pickety" pieces:

- Hickety Pickety black hen
- Nest with one egg and nest with ten eggs OR folding 1-to-10 egg piece (see pattern and instructions on page 53)
- "Hickety Pickety" poster

If using the nest and egg punch-out pieces, arrange them in order of appearance before the audience arrives. If using the folding egg (see page 53), accordion-fold the egg piece so that it looks like a single egg.

Before sharing the rhyme, place the poster on an easel so the audience can see it clearly. Hold Hickety Pickety in one hand as you sing or say the rhyme, and with the other hand produce either the nest with its single egg OR the folded egg as you say "she lays eggs." Affix the hen to a large Velcro or magnet board so that your hands will be free to count the eggs and/or to open and close the folding egg piece. Hold up one finger next to the "one" egg, then either produce the nest with ten eggs OR dramatically open the folded egg for "ten." Count the ten eggs together with the audience the first time you produce them. If you wish to incorporate motions, you can lead the audience in the actions while still holding and manipulating the nests or the folding egg due to their relatively small size.

Utilize the sections of Mother Goose Rhyme Time that work best for you and your storytime group or classroom. Experiment with new ideas and techniques. Practice ahead of time so you feel comfortable with the material and can focus on the audience rather than on trying to remember how you intended to share the rhyme.

Storytime

Share "Hickety Pickety" as a song or as a chant; bouncing, patting your lap, or clapping to keep a rhythm. Sing or say the rhyme quickly and slowly, loudly and quietly. Add movements and chicken noises as desired. Encourage the children's caregivers to adapt motions or make up new ones as appropriate for their child; many different actions are possible. Here are a few options:

Babies (*Sitting on caregivers' laps*)

Hickety Pickety, my black hen,
(*Bounce baby or bicycle baby's legs.*)
She lays eggs for women and men.
Sometimes ONE,
(*Hold up one finger.*)
And sometimes TEN!
(*Hold up ten fingers.*)
Hickety Pickety, my black hen.
(*Bounce baby or bicycle baby's legs.*)

Older Children (*Standing or sitting*)

Hickety Pickety, my black hen,
(*Clap or pat lap rhythmically.*)
She lays eggs for women and men.
(*Flap wings and "bawk-bawk."*)
Sometimes ONE,
(*Hold up one finger.*)
And sometimes TEN!
(*Hold up ten fingers.*)
Hickety Pickety, my black hen.
(*Clap or pat lap rhythmically.*)

Early Literacy Activities

Consider integrating one or several of the activities or techniques suggested below as you share the nursery rhyme. All activities should be approached in a fun and playful manner,

encouraging curiosity and allowing for children's individual differences. **Note:** Be aware of children's developmental stages and focus on the activities that are appropriate for the ages and stages of your group. The suggestions provided are intended to give you a variety of ideas to work with over time. You will not incorporate all of the techniques at once. Share one rhyme several times during a single storytime, and repeat the same rhyme over several storytimes. Try different activities to highlight a different skill during each storytime.

Print Motivation (*Encourage interest in and excitement about reading and books.*)

- Say the words rhythmically and with enthusiasm, conveying your enjoyment of the rhyme.

- Repeat the rhyme several times together with the children, encouraging their own enjoyment and internalization of its lively rhythms.

Language and Vocabulary (*Introduce and explain new words or new meanings to familiar words.*)

- Use the rhyme pieces to illustrate and help explain language and vocabulary. Say: "Here is Hickety Pickety (*point to the hen*). Hickety Pickety is the hen's name. A hen is a grown-up girl chicken. What color is Hickety Pickety? Black. She lays eggs (*hold up the folded egg OR the cluster of ten eggs in their nest*) for women and men. Sometimes she lays one (*hold up one finger*) egg (*point to the single egg in its nest OR to the folded egg*), and sometimes she lays ten (*hold up ten fingers*) eggs (*point to the ten eggs in their nest and count them together OR open the folded egg and count the eggs together*)."

- Talk or sing about the illustrations: "I see a hen." "I see a nest." Pause for the children to name the object to which you are pointing: "I see a _____." Expand on descriptive features of the illustrations to build vocabulary and encourage the children's awareness of and attention to details: "I see a hen. A hen with black feathers and yellow feet."

Phonological Awareness *(Play with rhymes, practice breaking words apart and putting them back together, and listen for beginning sounds and alliteration.)*

- Play with the words and animals in the rhyme and change them. Use puppets or props to dramatize. For example:

  Hickety Pickety, my little dog,
  He goes with me when I jog.
  In the rain,
  And through the fog!
  Hickety Pickety, my little dog.

- Explain that rhyming words sound the same at the end. "Dog" and "jog" and "fog" all rhyme. Try pausing just before the end of a rhyming pair and encourage the children to supply the rhyming word (such as "jog" and "fog" above) with the support of visual clues or context, or simply through the sounds suggested by the rhyme.

- Play an "oddity task" game. For example, which word does not rhyme? Hen, eggs, ten. *(Answer: eggs.)* Which word sounds different at the beginning? Hickety, hen, for. *(Answer: for.)* Which word sounds different at the end? Lays, men, eggs. *(Answer: men.)*

- Blend word parts in a variety of ways.

  Syllables: some ... times. What's the word? *(Sometimes.)*

  Onset sound: /m/ ... en. What's the word? *(Men.)* What other words start with /m/?

  Phoneme by phoneme (for older children, in primary grades): /h/-/e/-/n/. What's the word? *(Hen.)*

- Practice segmenting or "stretching" the nursery rhyme words (for older children, in primary grades). Show the children a rubber band and stretch it out and in. As you stretch the rubber band out longer, you can see all of its parts more clearly. Explain that you can also stretch words, so that you can hear each individual sound (phoneme) in the word. Stretch the word "ten": /t/-/e/-/n/. Sometimes one phoneme is represented by more than one letter, such as in

the word "eggs": /e/-/gg/-/s/. "Eggs" contains three phonemes. Stretch other nursery rhyme words.

- Clap words: Clap once for each word in the rhyme, following the poster. Introduce variety by stomping feet or jumping once for each word.

- Clap syllables: Older children can learn to clap once for each syllable in the rhyme. Practice with one word at a time as the children begin to understand the concept. For example: Hick-e-ty (3 claps); Pick-e-ty (3 claps); my (1 clap); black (1 clap); hen (1 clap); She (1 clap); lays (1 clap); eggs (1 clap); for (1 clap); wom-en (2 claps); and (1 clap); men (1 clap). Introduce variety by stomping feet or jumping to the syllables.

Print Awareness *(Notice print and know how to handle books and follow the written word on a page.)*

- Point to the "Hickety Pickety" poster. Say: "Our nursery rhyme is written right up here. I'll read it aloud, and then we'll say it again together." Follow the text of the rhyme with your finger as you read the poster, from left to right.

- Occasionally turn the poster upside down or sideways and see if the children detect the problem.

Narrative Skills *(Practice retelling stories or events, sequencing the order in which events happened, and adding descriptions.)*

- Talk and ask two or three open-ended questions about the rhyme and the objects and characters in it, and allow the children to ask questions. Avoid asking yes/no questions unless there is a specific purpose in doing so. Qualify questions by including the phrase "do you think," as in "Why do you think ...?" or "What do you think ...?" This type of question does not have a "right" answer that children are afraid they will get wrong. For example: Why do you think Hickety Pickety lays different numbers of eggs? Do you think that she lay eggs for anyone else besides women and men? If yes, who? Do you think she sometimes lays eggs for children?

- If you have a small enough group and adequate time, act out "Hickety Pickety" with creative dramatics. Make a giant nest from twisted blankets or a large round plastic tub. Have several children at a time be Hickety Pickety, wearing their feather hats (see Additional Extension Ideas below), while the others are the "women and men." Have two egg baskets for the Hickety Pickety children to fill with plastic eggs. When you get to the number part of the rhyme, say the number that is in each basket, such as: "Sometimes THREE, And sometimes EIGHT!" Make sure that each child gets to play both the "Hickety Pickety" and the "women and men" roles.

Letter Knowledge—Letter P *(Learn to recognize and identify letters, knowing that they have different names and sounds and that the same letter can look different.)*

- Show a large size cutout or magnet-backed foam letter "P" and "p" (see Resources). Point to the capital "P" letter that begins the word "Pickety" in the title of your poster. Say: "Here is the letter P—a big uppercase, or capital P." Draw the capital letter "P" in the air as a group. Point to a small letter "p" on the poster within the rhyme's text. Say: "Here is also the letter p—a small, lowercase p." Draw a lowercase "p" in the air as a group. Make the /P/ sound and say: "P is for Pickety; P is for Pizza; P is for Paint; P is for Pool; P is for Please; P is for Pie." Encourage the audience to repeat each phrase after you. Include three or four examples.

- Demonstrate making the shapes of "P" and "p" using string or pipe cleaners.

Parent/Caregiver Connection

- Reinforce the parent/caregiver's key role in their child's early literacy development through comfortable, relaxed times together with songs, rhymes, and books. Emphasize fun and enjoyment as the goals.

- Encourage caregivers to participate during storytime and to incorporate "Hickety Pickety" at home during play and reading

times. Select one of the "Hickety Pickety" early literacy activities that you share together during storytime, and briefly explain how the activity supports children's early literacy development. Suggest repeating the activity at home. Try different activities to highlight different skills during each storytime.

- Share information about Dialogic, or "Hear and Say" Reading (see Resources). Encourage parents and caregivers to individually discuss the day's rhyme, its characters, and events in an open-ended way with their children, following the child's interest while affirming and expanding upon their answers. For example, point to the hen Hickety Pickety in "Hickety Pickety" and ask, "What is this?" Child: "A hen." Follow up with positive affirmation, and enlarge: "Yes, it's a hen named Hickety Pickety. What do you notice about this hen?" Child: "Black." Expand: "Yes, the hen's feathers are black." Help the child repeat longer phrases. Ask open-ended questions such as: "What do you see in this picture?" Build on the things that catch the child's interest. This type of positive, interactive discussion around familiar rhymes and books helps improve early language development, communication, and parent/child relationships.

Take-home "Hickety Pickety"

Copy the "Hickety Pickety" illustrations from page 54 onto card stock and distribute. Color, cut out, and assemble the pieces at the end of storytime, or encourage the families to do so at home. Make a sample of the take-home version, and demonstrate singing or saying the rhyme using the small pieces. (Families may affix sticky-back magnet material to pieces for playtime use on a magnetic surface such as a cookie sheet or the refrigerator if desired. Be aware of choking hazard considerations for younger children.)

Additional Extension Ideas

Note: For all craft activities, provide materials for adult attendees as well as children. Encourage children and adults to talk together

about what they are making, and to use the completed crafts to retell or act out the rhyme.

- Show the pictures from several different nursery rhyme books that illustrate "Hickety Pickety" and repeat the rhyme together with each new illustration. Talk about the differences between the various illustrations.

- Cut out 19 individual card stock eggs and affix a Velcro dot or sticky magnet to each to play a numbers game. Line up ten of the eggs along the bottom of a Velcro or magnet board, and place four eggs in a line above them. Say the rhyme changing the numbers, "... sometimes FOUR, and sometimes TEN!" and so forth.

- Talk about: What other creatures lay eggs? Turtles, butterflies, ducks, fish, snakes, and so forth. How long do the various eggs take to hatch? Do they need to be sat upon or kept warm to hatch?

- Make Hickety Pickety feather hats. Glue black craft feathers to the bottom side of a regular-sized paper plate. Paper punch a hole in each side of the hat, and tie black yarn or elastic through the holes to make a chin strap.

- Cut out Hickety Pickety hen shapes from black card stock or construction paper and decorate them with black craft feathers, google eyes, yellow construction paper beaks, and yellow pipe cleaner feet.

- Make an egg-laying Hickety Pickety hen from a Styrofoam or paper cup. Glue craft feathers, eyes, a beak, comb, and wattle to the upside-down cup to make Hickety Pickety. Give each child plastic Easter eggs to hide under their Hickety Pickety cup. Say the rhyme as you lift the hen to reveal its magically appearing eggs.

- Make an Egg-Laying Black Hen. Complete instructions are included in the book *Crafts From Your Favorite Nursery Rhymes* by Kathy Ross (Millbrook Press, 2002).

- Make a large egg-laying Hen Box Puppet, and have the children make small-size Hen Tube Puppets that lay jelly bean eggs. Complete instructions are included in *A Pocketful of Puppets: Mother Goose* by Tamara Hunt and Nancy Renfro (Nancy Renfro Studios, 1998).

- Talk about the various colors and breeds of chickens in real life: white, brown, red, black, speckled. Look at the beautiful photographs in various chicken breed coffee table books, such as Stephen Green-Armytage's *Extraordinary Chickens* (H. N. Abrams, 2000) and *Extra Extraordinary Chickens* (H. N. Abrams, 2005). Encourage the children to identify the kind of chicken they think Hickety Pickety might be.

- Imagine together what wild colors or prints chickens could be for pretend (blue, green, purple, pink, striped, spotted, plaid, etc.). Cut out differently colored or printed hen shapes and write the color's name on each of them. Hold each hen up one at a time, saying the rhyme with the different colors or prints.

- Read *Big Fat Hen* illustrated by Keith Baker (Harcourt Brace, 1994). Big Fat Hen counts to ten with her hen friends and all of their baby chicks.

- Make the shapes of "P" and "p" using string, pipe cleaners, or clay.

Hickety Pickety

Merrily

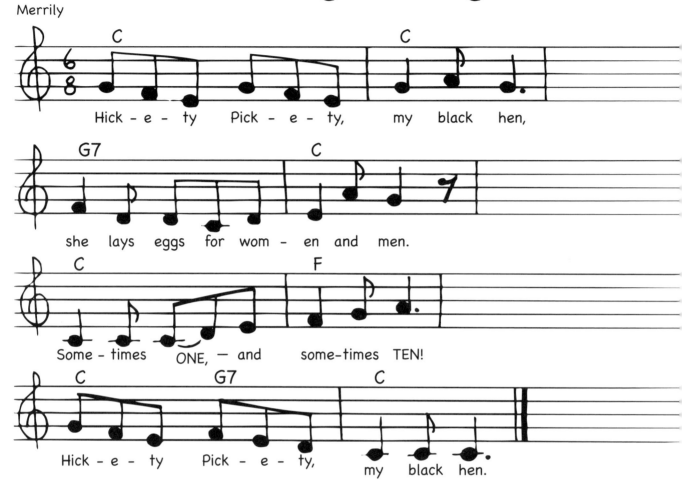

Hick – e – ty Pick – e – ty, my black hen,

she lays eggs for wom – en and men.

Some – times ONE, — and some-times TEN!

Hick – e – ty Pick – e – ty, my black hen.

Hickety Pickety Folding 1-to-10 Egg Pattern

1. Cut a strip of white paper 31¼" long by 5½" wide. (Fadeless white roll paper works well.) Accordion-fold the strip at 3 ⅛" intervals (see the folding template below), so that you have ten folded panels.

2. Photocopy the egg pattern below and cut it out. Trace the egg outline on the front panel of the folded strip.

3. Cutting through all of the folded layers, cut the rounded egg top and egg bottom. Make sure to leave the two flat sides attached!

4. Open your folding egg and make sure that there are ten egg panels before using!

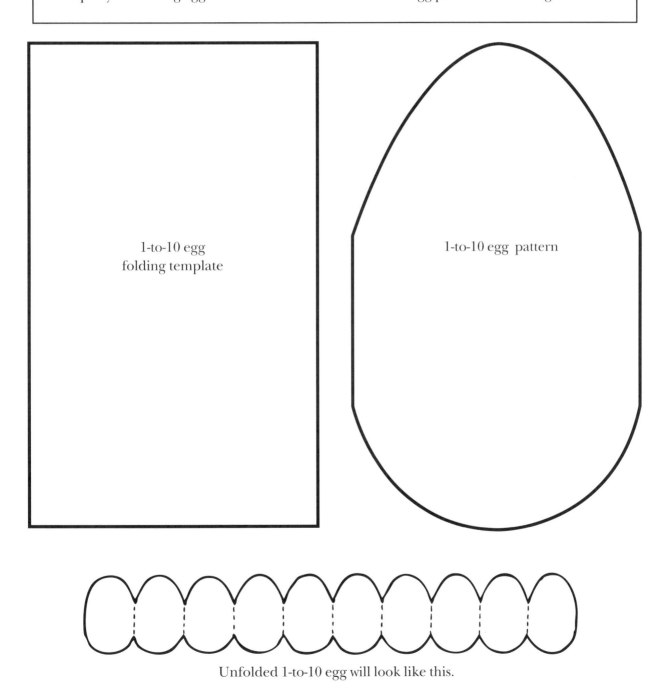

1-to-10 egg
folding template

1-to-10 egg pattern

Unfolded 1-to-10 egg will look like this.

Take-home Hickety Pickety

Hickety Pickety, my black hen,

She lays eggs for women and men.

Sometimes ONE,

And sometimes TEN!

Hickety Pickety, my black hen.

Hickory Dickory Dock

Hickory dickory dock,

The mouse ran up the clock.

The clock struck one,

The mouse ran down,

Hickory dickory dock.

Variants

A common variant is "The clock struck one, And down he run." Some performers such as Priscilla Hegner add the phrase "tick-tock" after the first, second, and last lines.

Additional lyrics have been added such as "The clock struck three, The mouse ran away"; and "The clock struck ten, The mouse came again" in Rimbault's *Nursery Rhymes with the Tunes to Which they Are Still Sung* (1846). Recent adaptations include the following verses on Priscilla Hegner's sound recording *Teach A Toddler: Playful Songs for Learning* (Kimbo Educational, 1985):

> The clock struck two, / The mouse said, "Boo!"
>
> The clock struck three, / The mouse said, "Whee!"
>
> The clock struck four, / The mouse said, "No more!"

History

Historically used by children as a "counting-out" rhyme to determine the leader for a game, the rhyme's rhythm beautifully imitates the sound of a pendulum clock. The words "Hickory dickory dock" echo the numbers eight, nine, and ten in the way that Westmoreland, England, shepherds counted for centuries: "hevera," "devera," "dick."

Musical Notation

See musical notation on page 60.

Preparing and Using the Mother Goose Rhyme Time Pieces

"Hickory Dickory Dock" pieces:

- Tall clock with movable hour and minute hands

- Mouse (affix to a wooden craft stick if desired)

- "Hickory Dickory Dock" poster

Make sure the clock rhyme piece's hands are set to almost one o'clock before the audience arrives. The mouse may be used exactly as it is and held in your hand, or it may be glued or taped securely to a wooden craft stick to create a mouse stick puppet.

Before sharing the rhyme, place the poster on an easel so the audience can see it clearly. Hold the clock in one hand as you say or sing the rhyme, or affix it to a large Velcro or magnet board. Run the mouse up the clock with the other hand and hold up one finger as the clock strikes "one," then run the mouse back down the clock. If you wish to incorporate motions, you can lead the audience in the actions while still holding and manipulating the mouse.

Utilize the sections of Mother Goose Rhyme Time that work best for you and your storytime group or classroom. Experiment with new ideas and techniques. Practice ahead of time so you feel comfortable with the material and can focus on the audience rather than on trying to remember how you intended to share the rhyme.

Storytime

Share "Hickory Dickory Dock" as a song or as a chant; bouncing, patting your lap, or clapping to keep a rhythm. Sing or say the rhyme quickly and slowly, loudly and quietly. Add movements and squeaking mouse noises as desired. Encourage the children's caregivers to adapt motions or make up new ones as appropriate for their child; many different actions are possible. Here are a few options:

Babies (*Sitting on caregivers' laps*)

> Hickory dickory dock,
> (*Bounce baby on knee.*)
> The mouse ran up the clock.
> (*Bounce baby over to other knee OR run fingers up baby's arm to tickle neck.*)
> The clock struck one,
> (*Hold up one finger.*)
> The mouse ran down,
> (*Bounce baby back to the other knee OR run fingers back down baby's arm.*)
> Hickory dickory dock.
> (*Bounce baby on knee.*)

Older Children (*Standing or sitting*)

> Hickory dickory dock,
> (*Clap hands rhythmically.*)
> The mouse ran up the clock.
> (*Lift arms up in the air.*)
> The clock struck one,
> (*Hold up one finger high over head.*)
> The mouse ran down,
> (*Drop arms to clap knees on "down."*)
> Hickory dickory dock.
> (*Clap hands rhythmically.*)

Early Literacy Activities

Consider integrating one or several of the activities or techniques suggested below as you share the nursery rhyme. All activities should be approached in a fun and playful manner, encouraging curiosity and allowing for children's individual differences. **Note:** Be aware of children's developmental stages and focus on the activities that are appropriate for the ages and stages of your group. The suggestions provided are intended to give you a variety of ideas to work with over time. You will not incorporate all of the techniques at once. Share one rhyme several times during a single storytime, and repeat the same rhyme over several storytimes. Try different activities to highlight a different skill during each storytime.

Print Motivation (*Encourage interest in and excitement about reading and books.*)

- Say the words rhythmically and with enthusiasm, conveying your enjoyment of the rhyme.

- Repeat the rhyme several times together with the children, encouraging their own enjoyment and internalization of its lively rhythms.

Language and Vocabulary (*Introduce and explain new words or new meanings to familiar words.*)

- Use the rhyme pieces to illustrate and help explain language and vocabulary. Say: "The words 'Hickory dickory dock' are silly nonsense, but they were probably put into this rhyme because they sound like the tick-tocking of a great big clock. The mouse (*point to or hold up the mouse*) runs up (*move the mouse up the side of the clock as though he is running*) the clock (*point to the clock*). When the clock strikes one (*adjust the clock's hands so it says one o'clock*), that means the clock announces that it is one o'clock by going 'bong!' or making some other noise. Then the mouse runs back down (*run the mouse back down the clock*) the clock."

- Talk or sing about the illustrations: "I see a clock." "I see a mouse." Pause for the children to name the object to which you are pointing: "I see a _____." Expand on descriptive features of the illustrations to

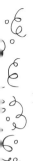

build vocabulary and encourage the children's awareness of and attention to details: "I see a mouse. A small gray mouse with big pink ears."

Phonological Awareness *(Play with rhymes, practice breaking words apart and putting them back together, and listen for beginning sounds and alliteration.)*

- Play with the words, creatures, and objects in the rhyme and change them. Use puppets or props to dramatize. For example:

  Hickory dickory duck,
  The duck is driving a truck!
  The truck got stuck,
  In yucky muck,
  Hickory dickory duck.

- Explain that rhyming words sound the same at the end. "Dock" and "clock" rhyme; and "duck," "truck," "stuck," and "muck" all rhyme. Try pausing just before the end of a rhyming pair and encourage the children to supply the rhyming word (such as "truck," "stuck," "muck," and "duck") with the support of visual clues or context, or simply through the sounds suggested by the rhyme.

- Blend word parts in a variety of ways.

  <u>Syllables:</u> hick ... o ... ry. What's the word? *(Hickory.)*

  <u>Onset sound:</u> /d/ ... own. What's the word? *(Down.)* What other words start with /d/?

  <u>Phoneme by phoneme (for older children, in primary grades):</u> /r/-/a/-/n/. What's the word? *(Ran.)*

- Practice segmenting or "stretching" the nursery rhyme words (for older children, in primary grades). Show the children a rubber band and stretch it out and in. As you stretch the rubber band out longer, you can see all of its parts more clearly. Explain that you can also stretch words, so that you can hear each individual sound (phoneme) in the word. Stretch the word "up": /u/-/p/. Sometimes one phoneme is represented by more than one letter, such as in the word "dock": /d/-/o/-/ck/. "Dock" contains

three phonemes. Stretch other nursery rhyme words.

- Clap words: Clap once for each word in the rhyme, following the poster. Introduce variety by stomping feet or jumping once for each word.

- Clap syllables: Older children can learn to clap once for each syllable in the rhyme. Practice with one word at a time as the children begin to understand the concept. For example: Hick-or-y (3 claps); dick-or-y (3 claps); dock (1 clap); The (1 clap); mouse (1 clap); ran (1 clap); up (1 clap); the (1 clap); clock (1 clap). Introduce variety by stomping feet or jumping to the syllables.

Print Awareness *(Notice print and know how to handle books and follow the written word on a page.)*

- Point to the "Hickory Dickory Dock" poster. Say: "Our nursery rhyme is written right up here. I'll read it aloud, and then we'll say it again together." Follow the text of the rhyme with your finger as you read the poster, from left to right.

- Occasionally turn the poster upside down or sideways and see if the children detect the problem.

Narrative Skills *(Practice retelling stories or events, sequencing the order in which events happened, and adding descriptions.)*

- Talk and ask two or three open-ended questions about the rhyme and the objects and characters in it, and allow the children to ask questions. Avoid asking yes/no questions unless there is a specific purpose in doing so. Qualify questions by including the phrase "do you think," as in "Why do you think ...?" or "What do you think ...?" This type of question does not have a "right" answer that children are afraid they will get wrong. For example: Why do you think the mouse ran up the clock? Why do you think the mouse ran back down the clock again? What do you think it sounded like to his little mouse ears when the clock struck one o'clock? Where do you think the mouse is going after he runs down the clock again? What do you do at special times during the day?

- If you have a small enough group and adequate time, act out "Hickory Dickory Dock" with "Clock and Mouse Costumes" (see Additional Extension Ideas below).

Letter Knowledge—Letter H (*Learn to recognize and identify letters, knowing that they have different names and sounds and that the same letter can look different.*)

- Show a large-size cutout or magnet-backed foam letter "H" and "h" (see Resources). Point to the capital "H" letters that begin the word "Hickory" in the title of your poster. Say: "Here is the letter H—a big uppercase, or capital H." Draw the capital letter "H" in the air as a group. Point to a small letter "h" on the poster within the rhyme's text. Say: "Here is also the letter h—a small, lowercase h." Draw a lowercase "h" in the air as a group. Make the breathy /H/ sound and say: "H is for Hickory; H is for Hi; H is for Hop; H is for House; H is for Hat; H is for Help; H is for Horse; H is for Head; H is for Hand; H is for Hiccup; H is for Happy." Encourage the audience to repeat each phrase after you. Include three or four examples.

- Demonstrate making the shapes of "H" and "h" using string or pipe cleaners.

Parent/Caregiver Connection

- Reinforce the parent/caregiver's key role in their child's early literacy development through comfortable, relaxed times together with songs, rhymes, and books. Emphasize fun and enjoyment as the goals.

- Encourage caregivers to participate during storytime and incorporate "Hickory Dickory Dock" at home during play and reading times. Select one of the "Hickory Dickory Dock" early literacy activities that you share together during storytime, and briefly explain how the activity supports children's early literacy development. Suggest repeating the activity at home. Try different activities to highlight different skills during each storytime.

- Share information about Dialogic, or "Hear and Say" Reading (see Resources).

Encourage parents and caregivers to individually discuss the day's rhyme, its characters, and events in an open-ended way with their children, following the child's interest while affirming and expanding upon their answers. For example, point to the mouse in "Hickory Dickory Dock" and ask, "What is this?" Child: "A mouse." Follow up with positive affirmation, and enlarge: "Yes, it's a little gray mouse with big pink ears. What do you notice about the mouse?" Child: "Tail." Expand: "Yes, the mouse has a long pink tail that curls up at the end." Help the child repeat longer phrases. Ask open-ended questions such as: "What do you see in this picture?" Build on the things that catch the child's interest. This type of positive, interactive discussion around familiar rhymes and books helps improve early language development, communication, and parent/child relationships.

Take-home "Hickory Dickory Dock"

Copy the "Hickory Dickory Dock" illustrations from page 61 onto card stock and distribute. Color, cut out, and assemble the pieces at the end of storytime, or encourage the families to do so at home. Affix the mouse to a wide craft stick as a stick puppet if desired. Make a sample of the take-home version, and demonstrate singing or saying the rhyme using the small pieces. (Families may affix sticky-back magnet material to pieces for playtime use on a magnetic surface such as a cookie sheet or the refrigerator if desired. Be aware of choking hazard considerations for younger children.)

Additional Extension Ideas

Note: For all craft activities, provide materials for adult attendees as well as children. Encourage children and adults to talk together about what they are making, and to use the completed crafts to retell or act out the rhyme.

- Show the pictures from several different nursery rhyme books that illustrate "Hickory Dickory Dock" and repeat the rhyme together with each new illustration. Talk about the differences between the various illustrations.

- Practice counting like a mouse, using a squeaky voice and squeaking in between numbers. "1 squeak, 2 squeak, 3 squeak," and so forth. Practice counting like other animals, using gruff, ribbiting, growling voices.

- Make "Hickory Dickory Dock" grandfather clocks from card stock or poster board, and paper punch a small hole near the top of each clock. Tie a small card stock mouse to one end of a piece of yarn and thread the yarn through the hole. When the yarn is pulled from the back, the mouse scurries up the clock. When the clock strikes one, pull the mouse back down.

- Make Hickory Dickory Mouse stick puppets. Cut out card stock half-heart shapes for the mice bodies and draw eyes and whiskers at the pointed ends to create faces. Glue on ears, yarn tails, and pom-pom noses. Affix the mice to craft sticks with glue or double-stick tape. Say the rhyme for each child's mouse as the child manipulates it. For example:

  Hickory dickory dock,
  The mouse ran up the chair.
  The clock struck one,
  The mouse ran down,
  Hickory dickory dock.

- Make clock faces from paper plates. Cut out card stock hour and minute hands ahead of time and make a small slit near the bottom of each through which to affix a metal brad fastener or knotted yarn. Provide number stickers for the clock, or help the children write the numbers. Provide sample clocks so they can see the numbers' placement. Practice some rudimentary telling-time skills as a group.

- Using your paper plate clock face as a visual aid, repeat the "Hickory Dickory Dock" rhyme for each number on the clock. For example:

  Hickory dickory dock,
  The mouse ran up the clock.
  The clock struck two,
  The mouse ran down,
  Hickory dickory dock.

Proceed with the numbers in numerical order at first, but as the children become familiar with the game try mixing the numbers around.

- Make a Run Around the Clock craft. Draw a running mouse on the top edge of a piece of card stock paper and outline a long, wide tab of blank paper below it that is slightly longer than the radius of the paper plate. If you hold the mouse so it shows above the edge of the paper plate, the tab should reach slightly past the plate's center. Cut out the mouse with the long tab. Punch a small hole in the middle of the paper plate and near the bottom of the tab. Insert a metal brad fastener or knotted yarn through the plate and tab, so the mouse can run around the clock.

- Make "Hickory Dickory" lace-up mice. Cut out a construction paper heart with the paper folded in half so both halves of the heart match exactly. Paper punch evenly spaced holes along the outer curved edge of the heart. Begin lacing the mouse together at the pointed (nose) end, and continue until about two-thirds done. Stuff the mouse body with fiberfill or bits of crumpled paper and finish lacing. Tie off the yarn at the back end of the mouse, leaving a length of yarn for the mouse's tail. Add felt or paper ears, a pom-pom nose, eyes, and whiskers.

- Make a Clock and Mouse Costume. Complete instructions are included in *Crafts From Your Favorite Nursery Rhymes* by Kathy Ross (Millbrook Press, 2002).

- Read *The Completed Hickory Dickory Dock* by Jim Aylesworth (Atheneum, 1990). Completes the classic nursery rhyme about the mouse that ran up the clock.

- Make the shapes of "H" and "h" using string, pipe cleaners, or clay.

Hickory Dickory Dock

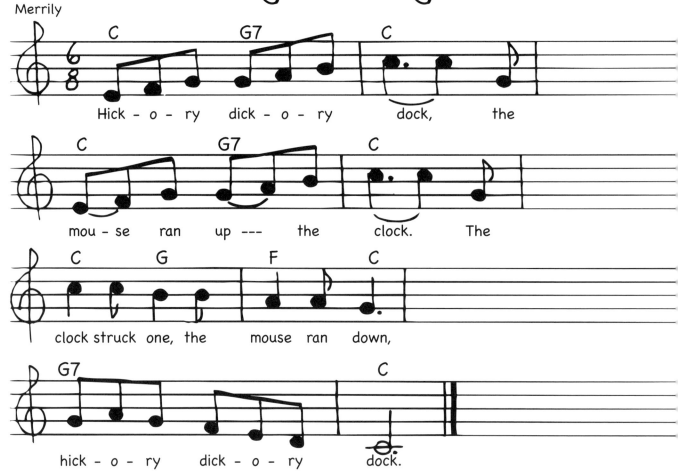

Merrily

C   **G7**   **C**

Hick - o - ry   dick - o - ry   dock,   the

C   **G7**   **C**

mou - se   ran   up ---   the   clock.   The

C   **G**   **F**   **C**

clock struck one, the   mouse ran   down,

G7   **C**

hick - o - ry   dick - o - ry   dock.

Take-home Hickory Dickory Dock

Hickory dickory dock,

The mouse ran up the clock.

The clock struck one,

The mouse ran down,

Hickory dickory dock.

Bibliographies and Resources

Mother Goose Collections to Share and Recommend

Alderson, Brian (sel.). *Cakes and Custard.* William Morrow & Co., 1975, 1974.

Crews, Nina. *The Neighborhood Mother Goose.* Greenwillow Books, 2004.

dePaola, Tomie. *Tomie dePaola's Mother Goose.* Putnam, 1985.

Engelbreit, Mary. *Mary Engelbreit's Mother Goose: One Hundred Best-Loved Verses.* HarperCollins, 2005.

Foreman, Michael. *Michael Foreman's Mother Goose.* Harcourt, 1991.

Hoberman, Mary Ann. *You Read to Me, I'll Read to You: Very Short Mother Goose Tales to Read Together.* Little, Brown and Company, 2005.

Kubler, Annie, illus. *Pat-a-Cake!: Nursery Rhymes.* Child's Play, 2005. (Board book)

Kubler, Annie, illus. *Peek-a-Boo!: Nursery Games.* Child's Play, 2005. (Board book)

Kubler, Annie, illus. *See-Saw! Nursery Songs.* Child's Play, 2005. (Board book)

Lansky, Bruce. *Mary Had a Little Jam and Other Silly Rhymes.* Meadowbrook Press, 2004. Reprint of *The New Adventures of Mother Goose: Gentle Rhymes for Happy Times* (1993).

Lobel, Arnold. *Arnold Lobel's Book of Mother Goose.* Knopf, 1997. Reprint of *The Random House Book of Mother Goose* (1986).

Long, Sylvia. *Sylvia Long's Mother Goose.* Chronicle Books, 1999.

Opie, Iona, ed. Illus. by Rosemary Wells. *My Very First Mother Goose.* Candlewick Press, 1996.

Opie, Iona, ed. Illus. by Rosemary Wells. *Here Comes Mother Goose.* Candlewick Press, 1999.

Scarry, Richard. *Richard Scarry's Best Mother Goose Ever.* Western Publishing Co., 1970, 1964.

Smith, Jessie Willcox. *The Jessie Willcox Smith Mother Goose.* Derrydale Books, 1986.

Wright, Blanche Fisher, illus. *The Real Mother Goose.* Checkerboard Press, 1944, 1916.

Yaccarino, Dan, illus. *Dan Yaccarino's Mother Goose.* Random House, 2004.

History of Nursery Rhymes

Baring-Gould, William S., and Cecil Baring-Gould. *The Annotated Mother Goose.* Crown Publishers, 1962.

Christensen, James C. *Rhymes & Reasons: An Annotated Collection of Mother Goose Rhymes.* The Greenwich Workshop Press, 1977.

Delamar, Gloria T. *Mother Goose: From Nursery to Literature.* McFarland, 1987.

Montgomery, Michael G., and Wayne Montgomery. *Over the Candlestick: Classic Nursery Rhymes and the Real Stories Behind Them.* Peachtree Publishers, 2002.

Opie, Iona and Peter, eds. *The Oxford Dictionary of Nursery Rhymes.* Clarendon Press, 1951.

Roberts, Chris. *Heavy Words Lightly Thrown: The Reason Behind the Rhyme.* Gotham Books, 2005.

Stevens, Albert Mason. *The Nursery Rhyme: Remnant of Popular Protest.* Coronado Press, 1968.

Thomas, K. E. *The Real Personages of Mother Goose.* Lothrop, Lee & Shepard, 1930.

Mother Goose Crafts

Cressy, Judith. *What Can You Do with a Paper Bag? Hats, Wigs, Masks, Crowns, Helmets, and Headdresses.* Chronicle Books, 2001.

Renfro, Nancy, and Tamara Hunt. *A Pocketful of Puppets: Mother Goose.* Nancy Renfro Studios, 1982.

Ross, Kathy. *Crafts From Your Favorite Children's Songs.* Millbrook Press, 2001.

Ross, Kathy. *Crafts From Your Favorite Nursery Rhymes.* Millbrook Press, 2002.

Ross, Kathy. *Crafts to Make in the Spring.* Millbrook Press, 1998.

Mother Goose Songbooks

Barratt, Carol. *The Mother Goose Songbook: Nursery Rhymes to Play and Sing.* Arranged for the piano by Carol Barratt. Derrydale Books, 1984.

Beall, Pamela Conn, and Susan Hagen Nipp. *Wee Sing Nursery Rhymes & Lullabies.* Price Stern Sloan, 2005, 2002, 1985.

Buck, Sir Percy. *The Oxford Nursery Song Book.* 3d ed. Oxford University Press, 1984, 1961, 1933.

Crane, Walter. *The Baby's Bouquet.* Robert Frederick Ltd., 1994. (First published in 1877.)

Crane, Walter. *The Baby's Opera.* Simon & Schuster, 1981. (First published in 1879.)

Larrick, Nancy, comp. *Songs from Mother Goose: With the Traditional Melody for Each.* Harper & Row, 1989.

Orth, L. E. *Sixty Songs from Mother Goose.* Set to music by L. E. Orth. Oliver Ditson Company, 1906.

Rey, H. A. *Humpty Dumpty: And Other Mother Goose Songs.* HarperFestival, 1995.

Sharon, Lois & Bram's Mother Goose. Little, Brown and Company, 1985.

Yolen, Jane. *Jane Yolen's Mother Goose Songbook.* Boyds Mills Press, 1992.

Yolen, Jane, ed. *This Little Piggy: And Other Rhymes to Sing and Play.* [Music CD included.] Candlewick Press, 2005.

Sound Recordings

Beall, Pamela Conn, and Susan Hagen Nipp. *Wee Sing Nursery Rhymes & Lullabies.* Price Stern Sloan, 2005, 2002, 1985.

The Countdown Kids. *Mommy and Me: Mary Had a Little Lamb.* Mommy and Me Enterprises, 1998.

The Countdown Kids. *Mommy and Me: Old MacDonald Had a Farm.* Mommy and Me Enterprises, 1998.

The Countdown Kids. *Mommy and Me: Rock-a-bye Baby.* Mommy and Me Enterprises, 1998.

The Countdown Kids. *Mommy and Me: Twinkle Twinkle Little Star.* Mommy and Me Enterprises, 1998.

Feldman, Jean. *Nursery Rhymes and Good Ol' Times with Dr. Jean.* Jean Feldman, 2002.

Hegner, Priscilla A. *Baby Games (6 Weeks - 1 Year).* Kimbo Educational, 1987.

Hegner, Priscilla, and Rose Grasselli. *Diaper Gym: Fun Activities for Babies on the Move.* Kimbo Educational, 1985.

Hegner, Priscilla. *Teach a Toddler: Playful Songs for Learning.* Kimbo Educational, 1985.

Jenkins, Ella. *Early, Early Childhood Songs.* Smithsonian Folkways Recordings, 1990.

Jenkins, Ella. *Nursery Rhymes: Rhyming and Remembering.* Smithsonian Folkways Recordings, 1974.

McGrath, Bob. *If You're Happy & You Know It ... Sing Along with Bob #1.* Bob's Kids Music, 1996, 1990.

McGrath, Bob, and Katharine Smithrim. *The Baby Record.* Bob's Kids Music, 2000.

McGrath, Bob, and Katharine Smithrim. *Songs & Games For Toddlers.* Bob's Kids Music, 2000.

Palmer, Hap. *Early Childhood Classics: Old Favorites With A New Twist.* Hap-Pal Music, Inc., 2000.

Palmer, Hap. *Hap Palmer Sings Classic Nursery Rhymes.* Educational Activities, Inc., 2003; Hap-Pal Music, Inc., 1991.

Raffi. *Singable Songs for the Very Young.* Troubador Records Ltd., 1976.

Sharon, Lois & Bram. *Mainly Mother Goose: Songs and Rhymes For Merry Young Souls.* Elephant Records, 1984.

Snee, Richard. *Mother Goose Rocks! Volume 1.* Boffomedia, Inc., 2000.

Sunseri, Mary Lee. *Mother Goose Melodies: Four & Twenty Olde Songs for Young Children.* Piper Grove, 2003.

Spanish Language Resources

Ada, Alma Flor, and F. Isabel Campoy. *Mama Goose: A Latino Nursery Treasury; Un Tesoro De Rimas Infantiles.* Illus. by Maribel Suarez. English editing by Tracy Hefferman. Hyperion, 2004.

Ada, Alma Flor, and F. Isabel Campoy, sel. *¡Pio Peep!: Traditional Spanish Nursery Rhymes.* English adapt. by Alice Schertle. Illus. by Vivi Escriva. HarperCollins, 2003. (Book and CD set: Rayo, 2006.)

Carlson, Ann, and Mary Carlson, illus. *Flannelboard Stories for Infants and Toddlers,* Bilingual Edition (Spanish-English). American Library Assn., 2005.

Hall, Nancy Abraham, and Jill Syverson-Stork, sel. and adapt. *Los Pollitos Dicen: Juegos, Rimas y Canciones Infantiles de Países de Habla Hispana; The Baby Chicks Sing: Traditional Games, Nursery Rhymes, and Lullabies from Spanish-Speaking Countries.* Illus. by Kay Chorao. Little, Brown and Company, 1994.

Orozco, Jose-Luis, sel., arr., and transl. *De Colores: and Other Latin-American Folk Songs for Children.* Illus. by Elisa Kleven. Dutton, 1994.

Orozco, Jose-Luis. *Jose-Luis Orozco Canta De Colores* [sound recording]. Arcoiris Records, 1996.

Orozco, Jose-Luis, sel., arr., and transl. *Diez Deditos; Ten Little Fingers & Other Play Rhymes and Action Songs from Latin America.* Illus. by Elisa Kleven. Dutton, 1997.

Orozco, Jose-Luis. *Diez Deditos* [sound recording]. Arcoiris Records, 1997.

Orozco, Jose-Luis. *Rin, Rin, Rin; Do, Re, Mi.* Illus. by David Diaz. Scholastic, 2005.

Orozco, Jose-Luis. *Rin, Rin, Rin; Do, Re, Mi* [sound recording]. Arcoiris Records, 2005.

See Jose-Luis Orozco's Web site at www.joseluis orozco.com for the following sound recordings and more:

Orozco, Jose-Luis. *Lirica Infantil volume #1: Latin American Children's Songs, Games and Rhymes.* Arcoiris Records.

Orozco, Jose-Luis. *Lirica Infantil volume #2: Latin American Children's Songs, Games and Rhymes.* Arcoiris Records.

Orozco, Jose-Luis. *Lirica Infantil volume #3: Latin American Children's Songs, Games and Rhymes.* Arcoiris Records.

Where to Buy Sound Recordings

Arcoiris Records (Jose-Luis Orozco)
P.O. Box 461900
Los Angeles, CA 90046
888.354.7373 phone / 310.659.4144 fax
www.joseluisorozco.com

Educational Record Center
3233 Burnt Mill Drive, Suite 100
Wilmington, NC 28403-2698
888.372.4543 phone / 888.438.1637 fax
www.erckids.com

Kimbo Educational
P.O. Box 477 J
Long Branch, NJ 07740
800.631.2187 phone / 732.870.3340 fax
www.Kimboed.com

Music for Little People
P.O. Box 1460
Redway, CA 95560-1460
707.923.3991 phone / 800.409.2457 phone
www.musicforlittlepeople.com

Where to Buy Alphabet Letters

Childcraft Education Corp.
P. O. Box 3239
Lancaster, PA 17604
800.631.5652 phone / 888.532.4453 fax
www.childcraft.com
(Jumbo 4.7" high UPPERCASE Letters, item #5G358374; Jumbo 4.3" high LOWERCASE Letters, item #5G358382)

Constructive Playthings
13201 Arrington Road
Grandview, MO 64030-1117
800.448.4115 phone / 816.761.9295 fax
www.cptoys.com
(Giant 4.75" Magnetic Foam UPPERCASE
Letters, item #EDL-776; Giant 4.75" Magnetic
Foam LOWERCASE Letters, item #EDL-617)
(Jumbo 7.5" Foam UPPERCASE Letters, item
#EDL-170; Jumbo 7.25" Foam LOWERCASE
Letters, item #EDL-171)

Highsmith Inc.
W5527 State Road 106
P.O. Box 800
Fort Atkinson, WI 53538-0800
800.558.2110 phone / 800.835.2329 fax
www.highsmith.com
(Durafoam Letters—6", 8", 10", and 12" high)

Lakeshore Learning Materials
2695 E. Dominguez Street
Carson, CA 90895
800.778.4456 phone / 800.537.5403 fax
www.lakeshorelearning.com
(Jumbo 5" Magnetic Letters—UPPERCASE,
item #RR932; Jumbo 5" Magnetic Letters—
LOWERCASE, item #RR933)

Storybook and Sound Recording Titles Listed in *Mother Goose Rhyme Time: Animals*

Aylesworth, Jim. *The Completed Hickory Dickory Dock*. Atheneum, 1990.

Baker, Keith. *Big Fat Hen*. Harcourt, 1994.

Denchfield, Nick. *Charlie the Chicken: A Pop-up Book*. Red Wagon Books, 1997.

Desmoinaux, Christel. *Mrs. Hen's Big Surprise*. Margaret K. McElderry Books, 2000.

Hegner, Priscilla. *Teach a Toddler: Playful Songs for Learning*. Kimbo Educational, 1985.

Hoberman, Mary Ann. *You Read to Me, I'll Read to You: Very Short Mother Goose Tales to Read Together*. Little, Brown and Company, 2005.

Hutchins, Pat. *The Wind Blew*. Macmillan, 1974.

Lord, John Vernon, and Janet Burroway. *The Giant Jam Sandwich*. Houghton Mifflin, 1973, 1972.

Raffi. *The Corner Grocery Store*. MCA Records, 1979.

Raffi. *Singable Songs for the Very Young*. Troubador Records Ltd., 1976.

Trapani, Iza (ret.). *Baa Baa Black Sheep*. Whispering Coyote, 2001.

Westcott, Nadine Bernard (illus.). *Peanut Butter & Jelly: A Play Rhyme*. Dutton Children's Books, 1993, 1987.

Mother Goose and Early Literacy Programming Books, Articles, and Video/DVDs

Briggs, Diane. *Toddler Storytime Programs*. Scarecrow Press, 1993.

Brown, Marc, coll. and illus. *Finger Rhymes*. Dutton, 1980.

Brown, Marc, coll. and illus. *Hand Rhymes*. Dutton, 1985.

Brown, Marc, coll. and illus. *Play Rhymes*. Dutton, 1987.

Butler, Dorothy. *Babies Need Books*. Atheneum, 1980.

Clow-Martin, Elaine. *Baby Games: The Joyful Guide to Child's Play from Birth to Three Years*. Rev. ed. Fitzhenry & Whiteside Ltd., 2003, Running Press, 1988.

Cobb, Jane. *I'm a Little Teapot! Presenting Preschool Storytime*. 2d ed. Black Sheep Pr., 1996.

Cobb, Jane. *What'll I Do with the Baby-oh? Nursery Rhymes, Songs and Stories for Babies*. Black Sheep Pr., 2006.

Cole, Joanna, and Stephanie Calmenson. *The Eentsy, Weentsy Spider; Fingerplays and Action Rhymes*. William Morrow, 1991.

Cole, Joanna, and Stephanie Calmenson. *Pat-A-Cake and Other Play Rhymes*. HarperCollins, 1992.

Davis, Robin Works. *Toddle On Over: Developing Infant & Toddler Literature Programs*. Alleyside Press, 1998.

De Salvo, Nancy. *Beginning with Books: Library Programming for Infants, Toddlers, and Preschoolers*. Library Professional Publications, 1993.

Diamant-Cohen, Betsy. "Mother Goose on the Loose: Applying Brain Research to Early Childhood Programs in the Public Library." *Public Libraries,* 43.1 (2004): 41–45.

Diamant-Cohen, Betsy, Ellen Riordan, and Regina Wade. "Make Way for Dendrites: How Brain Research Can Impact Children's Programming." *Children & Libraries,* 2.1 (2004): 12–20.

Diamant-Cohen, Betsy. *Mother Goose on the Loose.* Neal Schuman, 2006.

Ernst, Linda L. *Lapsit Services for the Very Young: A How-To-Do-It Manual.* Neal Schuman, 1995.

Ernst, Linda L. *Lapsit Services for the Very Young II: A How-To-Do-It Manual.* Neal Schuman, 2001.

Fehrenbach, Laurie A., and David P. Hurford, Carolyn R. Fehrenbach, and Rebecca Groves. "Developing the Emergent Literacy of Preschool Children through a Library Outreach Program." *Journal of Youth Services in Libraries,* 12:1 (1998): 40–1.

Ghoting, Saroj Nadkarni, and Pamela Martin-Diaz. *Early Literacy Storytimes @ Your Library: Partnering with Caregivers for Success.* American Library Assn., 2006.

Greene, Ellin. *Books, Babies, and Libraries.* American Library Assn., 1991.

Herb, Steve. "Building Blocks for Literacy: What Current Research Shows." *School Library Journal,* 43.7 (1997): 23.

Huebner, Colleen E. *Hear and Say Reading* [VHS or DVD]. Rotary Club of Bainbridge Island, 2001. (www.bainbridgeislandrotary.org)

Jeffery, Debby Ann. *Literate Beginnings: Programs for Babies and Toddlers.* American Library Assn., 1995.

Jeffery, Debby, and Ellen Mahoney. "Sitting Pretty: Infants, Toddlers, & Lapsits." *School Library Journal,* 35.8 (1989): 37–9.

Marino, Jane. "B Is for Baby, B Is for Books." *School Library Journal,* 43.3 (1997): 110–11.

Marino, Jane. *Babies in the Library!* Scarecrow Press, 2003.

Marino, Jane, and Dorothy F. Houlihan. *Mother Goose Time: Library Programs for Babies and Their Caregivers.* H. W., Wilson, 1992.

McGuiness, Diane. *Growing a Reader from Birth: Your Child's Path from Language to Literacy.* W. W. Norton & Co., 2004.

Nespeca, Sue McLeaf. "Bringing Up Baby." *School Library Journal,* 45, no. 11 (November 1999): 48-52.

Nespeca, Sue McLeaf. *Library Programming for Families with Young Children: A How-to-Do-It Manual.* Neal Schuman, 1994.

Neuman, Susan B. ed., et al. *Access for All: Closing the Book Gap for Children in Early Education.* International Reading Association, 2001.

Newcome, Zita. *Head, Shoulders, Knees, and Toes; and Other Action Rhymes.* Candlewick Press, 2002.

Nichols, Judy. *Storytimes for Two-Year-Olds.* 2d ed. American Library Assn., 1998.

Silberg, Jackie, and Pam Schiller, compilers. *The Complete Book of Rhymes, Songs, Poems, Fingerplays and Chants.* Gryphon House, 2002.

Walter, Virginia A. *Output Measures for Public Library Service to Children: A Manual of Standardized Procedures.* American Library Assn., 1992.

Wilner, Isabel, sel. *The Baby's Game Book.* Illus. by Sam Williams. Greenwillow Books, 2000.

Winkel, Lois, and Sue Kimmel. *Mother Goose Comes First: An Annotated Guide to the Best Books and Recordings for Your Preschool Child.* Henry Holt & Company, 1990.

Mother Goose Programming and Early Literacy Web Connections

America Reads Challenge
www.ed.gov/inits/americareads/index.html

Association of Library Service to Children: Born to Read: How to Raise a Reader
www.ala.org/ala/alsc/alscresources/bornto read/bornread.htm

Champaign Public Library (IL): Just for Kids: Mother Goose
www.champaign.org/kids/mgoose_tips.html

Children of the Code
www.childrenofthecode.org

Early Literacy and Brain Development
Resources (Saroj Ghoting)
www.earlylit.net/earlylit/bibliography.html

Every Child Ready to Read @ Your Library
www.pla.org/earlyliteracy.htm

Hennepin County Library (MN): Birth to Six
www.hclib.org/BirthTo6/

Mother Goose Society
www.librarysupport.net/mothergoosesociety/

Multnomah County (OR) Public Library: Early
Words
www.multcolib.org/birthtosix/

National Association of Education for the
Young Child
www.naeyc.org/

Nursery Rhymes at the Virtual Vine
www.thevirtualvine.com/nurseryrhymes.html

Project ECLIPSE: Mother Goose
eclipse.rutgers.edu/goose/literacy/

Public Library of Charlotte & Mecklenburg
County: Grow & Learn @ Your Library
www.plcmc.org/forKids/growlearn/

Reading Is Fundamental (RIF)
www.rif.org

A Rhyme a Week: Nursery Rhymes for Early
Literacy
curry.edschool.virginia.edu/go/wil/rimes_
and_rhymes.htm

West Bloomfield Township Public Library
(MI): Grow Up Reading @ the West Bloomfield
Township Public Library
www.growupreading.org

Zero to Three's Brain Wonders
www.zerotothree.org/brainwonders/